## "You can't get married without a groom," Grant said, shaking his head

Annie grabbed his arm, her fingers crumpling the sleeve of his tuxedo with desperation. "Please. You've got to help me. All you have to do is pretend to go through the ceremony as your brother. Then you can just drop me off at the airport and that will be the end of it." She paused and looked pleadingly up at him. "I just can't face this town as a deserted bride again."

Taking a step closer, she touched his chest, reminding him of the sizzling kiss they'd just shared. A kiss that struck Grant as far from brotherly.

*Damn.* "Okay," he said. "I'll play along."

Annie's face transformed into a dazzling smile. Before he could brace himself, she hugged him close, her body colliding with his, her curves reminding him how good it felt to hold her. Her musky scent whispered to him like a lover's invitation, and he felt the tug of desire. His gaze dropped to her mouth and he remembered how sweet and tempting she tasted.

"Thank you," she whispered before he could dip his head for another forbidden sample. "You won't regret this."

*But he already did.*

Dear Reader,

When I was a small child, my mother gave me a precious gift—the love of reading. While she sewed dresses for me, she read aloud my favorite stories, like *Go Dog Go*, over and over again as I turned the pages. When I became an adult, my sister suggested I should turn that "gift" into a profession—writing. And it's changed my life. Now that I'm a mother and a writer, I spend nap time and late night hours weaving stories. At all other waking moments, I am trying to pass the "gift" on to my two toddlers. I can't imagine a better life!

I'm especially thrilled to be part of the Get Caught Reading campaign, a national promotion created by North American publishers to encourage reading for the sheer pleasure of it. I'm sure my heroine, Annie Baxter, wouldn't mind being caught reading... but as the book opens, she's more worried about being caught without a groom! I hope you enjoy Annie's amorous adventures. And I hope even more that I've passed the "gift"—the love of reading—on to you.

Enjoy,

Leanna Wilson

## Books by Leanna Wilson

**HARLEQUIN TEMPTATION**
763—BACHELOR BLUES

**SILHOUETTE ROMANCE**
1305—HIS TOMBOY BRIDE
1378—BABIES, RATTLES AND CRIBS, OH MY!
1430—THE DOUBLE HEART RANCH
1484—THE THIRD KISS

# JUST SAY YES!
## Leanna Wilson

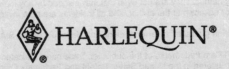

HARLEQUIN®

TORONTO • NEW YORK • LONDON
AMSTERDAM • PARIS • SYDNEY • HAMBURG
STOCKHOLM • ATHENS • TOKYO • MILAN • MADRID
PRAGUE • WARSAW • BUDAPEST • AUCKLAND

For Kathy, Frank, Jacob & Laura.
Thanks for all the love and support.

Thanks, Bob, for the information on New York!
Glad you're coming back to Texas!

ISBN 0-373-25931-X

JUST SAY YES!

Copyright © 2001 by Leanna Ellis.

All rights reserved. Except for use in any review, the reproduction or
utilization of this work in whole or in part in any form by any electronic,
mechanical or other means, now known or hereafter invented, including
xerography, photocopying and recording, or in any information storage
or retrieval system, is forbidden without the written permission of the
publisher, Harlequin Enterprises Limited, 225 Duncan Mill Road,
Don Mills, Ontario, Canada M3B 3K9.

All characters in this book have no existence outside the imagination of
the author and have no relation whatsoever to anyone bearing the same
name or names. They are not even distantly inspired by any individual
known or unknown to the author, and all incidents are pure invention.

This edition published by arrangement with Harlequin Books S.A.

® and TM are trademarks of the publisher. Trademarks indicated with
® are registered in the United States Patent and Trademark Office, the
Canadian Trade Marks Office and in other countries.

Visit us at www.eHarlequin.com

Printed in U.S.A.

# 1

"YOU SAW HIM?" Annie Baxter worried her bottom lip. "You're sure? Positive? No mistake?" She knew she sounded paranoid, but she'd earned the right.

"All tuxed out and ready to marry you." Aunt Maudie grinned, revealing a smear of hot-pink lipstick across her front tooth. She stuck one final bobby pin into Annie's blond hair to secure her veil then stepped back with a "Voila!"

Surveying the effects of the cascading veil, Annie felt a pinch in her chest. Would it really happen this time? Without a hitch? Maybe today she'd finally wed and be off to her new life.

Aunt Maudie fingered the satin trim along the veil and read Annie's expression in the mirror. "You don't like what I did with your hair?"

"No, no." She touched her wispy bangs and smoothed a lock behind her ear. She'd worn her hair in a pixie cut for years. There wasn't much that you could do to mess it up. Taking a tissue, she erased the lipstick off her aunt's enamel. "My hair's fine. This is simply...unbelievable." She took a steadying breath. "I can't believe it's really happening this time."

"Of course it's happening. Now quit your worrying. You need to stop listening to those old windbags in town. You should know it's only idle gossip."

But their words had prickly points that jabbed and

wounded. She'd been the headliner for the past three years.

Unfortunately, she'd given her nosy neighbors grist for their rumor mills. After all, she'd been jilted twice. Folks called her jinxed, and she'd been on the verge of believing them—until today.

Her groom was here. Griffin Thomas Stevens had arrived, ready and willing to marry her, to take her away from this dull town and insipid life!

It was her turn to have the last laugh. And she would, as she and her new husband peeled out of town on their way to their fabulous honeymoon in some romantic city—hopefully Paris or Rome. She wouldn't look in the rearview mirror at her hometown or the sad and humiliating memories that had trapped her here for too long.

"You are not the jinxed bride-to-be that everyone says." Maudie gave a curt nod, making her dyed platinum-blond hair bob around her flamboyant earrings. "That's pure nonsense."

Annie sank onto a velveteen chair in the corner of the bridal room at the Second Baptist Church of Lockett. She crossed her arms over the Hawaiian-print shirt she'd worn while her hair was being coiffed. She had a nightmare vision of living here the rest of her life in her parents' house as an old-maid schoolteacher. Kids would ask their folks why Miss Baxter was so tart, so irritable. "It's because she couldn't catch herself a husband," they'd say with a mixture of pity and sympathy.

*Well, just watch!*

One month ago when Griff had popped the question, she'd only half believed this day would arrive with church bells ringing and the organ playing the wedding march. The rock of a ring he'd given her hadn't convinced her of his intentions at first. She'd guarded her heart, protected herself from what she considered the inevitable—a man who'd get ice-cold feet. When he'd insisted they shop for her trousseau and pick out a china pattern, she'd begun to realize he was serious. With trepidation, she'd pulled her wedding dress out of storage.

Now here she was half dressed for the big event. Only an hour to go and she'd be Mrs. Griffin Stevens. It had only taken her thirty years and three grooms to get to this moment.

"Now," Aunt Maudie said, eyeing her gaudy watch that had more fake diamonds than a pawnshop, "let's get you into that fancy wedding gown."

Annie's stomach fluttered with sudden nerves and her mind spun with questions and doubts. She shoved them away. This was what she wanted; Griffin was the man for her. Wasn't he? How could a woman be sure?

*No, no, no.* She shook loose those thoughts. *I'm sure. I'm positive. I'm confident this is the right thing to do.*

She grabbed her aunt's hand. "What if something happens between now and the wedding?"

"What could happen?"

Annie laughed. "Anything! An earthquake could hit."

"In Texas?"

"There could be a flood."

"We're in the middle of a drought, sugar."

"Lightning could strike Griffin and kill him."

Maudie glanced out the window. "The sky's as blue as your eyes today."

"He could trip and get a concussion and forget all about me."

"Not likely."

Her real fear surfaced. "He could change his mind."

"You know what you need?" Aunt Maudie gave her hand a sympathetic squeeze.

"What?"

"French fries."

She laughed. "Now?"

"Not a better time. I'll run to the D-Q Palace and be right back. Nothing better than comfort food to get your mind off your worries. Then we'll get you all trussed up in that fancy gown."

Annie caught her aunt's mischievous grin. "That does sound tempting."

"It'll settle your stomach and calm your nerves." She scooped up her purse that resembled a city slicker's saddle and headed for the door. "This will be your last chance for the D-Q's finest greasiest fries. Nothing better."

"There are fast-food places in Dallas." In fact, the thought of one on every street corner made her almost giddy with excitement.

"Not the same." Aunt Maudie skimmed her hand down her curvaceous figure. "When you get to Dallas, you better be careful of eating too much fast food. Keep your figure, sugar. Men like a good bod."

"I'll remember that." Annie grinned, feeling light-hearted now and more optimistic that her wedding might actually take place.

"Remember, sugar, when you get a man, you have

to keep him happy." She gave a lascivious wink. "Know what I mean?"

Boy, did she! That's why she hadn't given in and had sex with Griffin before now. Her mother had always said, "Why buy the cow if you get the milk for free?" Convinced that having sex too early had been her mistake with her first two fiancés, Annie had tried a new tactic with Griffin. Now, tonight, she'd release all those natural urges and knock Griff's socks—and the rest of his clothes—off. It would be one heckuva night that would keep him grinning for weeks.

"I'll get into that fancy underwear you gave me while you're gone."

"It's called a garter and silk stockings, sugar." Her aunt gave a wink. "And trust me, men love 'em. Especially husbands!"

Aunt Maudie should know. She'd had six of her own. And reportedly a few that weren't hers in between.

But Annie planned to marry only once, for all eternity.

"WHO'S GOING to tell the bride the bad news?" Grant Stevens studied the other three groomsmen with slow deliberation, hoping one of them would be man enough to step forward.

Each of them wore the prescribed black tuxes for the supposedly joyous occasion, but from their deepening frowns they might as well have been at a funeral. All of them avoided Grant's hard stare. Beads of sweat dotted their foreheads. Grant's bow tie suddenly felt like a hangman's noose chafing his Adam's apple.

He'd been in the same situation twice before and it

didn't get any easier. If there was one positive thing about his parents being out of the country, it was that they weren't witnessing another Griffin debacle.

Thank God being a best man wasn't like acting as a second in a duel. He didn't have to step in and take the groom's place. No, dammit, he'd just get to shatter another bride's dream.

It was enough to reinforce Grant's determination to stay single. Hadn't he given the bad news to his brother's first fiancée and received a soggy, mascara-stained shirt in return? Then he'd delivered the blow to Griffin's second fiancée and received a broken nose for his trouble. Now his brother had jilted number three and Grant wanted to wipe his hands clean of the whole matrimonial farce. What was wrong with being a bachelor, with playing the field? It was his preference.

Like a pipe organ's chords silence resonated in the foyer of the church as Grant waited for a volunteer. The heat of the west Texas sun filtered through the stained-glass windows. Red, blue and green sunspots dotted the marble floor like confetti. Eager guests were filing into the chapel. Grant had called the three groomsmen over to a secluded corner for a huddle. A decision had to be made. Soon, before the wedding march began.

John Cummings shuffled his feet and scratched his receding hairline. "I wouldn't know what the hell to say."

Peter Rawlins ducked his head and mumbled, "Me, neither."

Eric Simmons crossed his arms over his chest. "The

groom's your brother, Grant. Don't you think you should handle it?"

"Diplomatically, of course," John offered, nodding his agreement.

"Cut right to the point and get it over with quick." Peter clapped Grant on the shoulder.

"Remind her she can keep the ring. That should alleviate some of the pain—" Eric cleared his throat "—and humiliation."

That had never worked before. Maybe Eric's perm had fried his brain. Grant clearly remembered the scar Griffin's last fiancée had pinned on the bridge of his nose with the engagement ring she'd kept.

He ground his teeth in anger. He wanted to wring his brother's neck for running out on his bride-to-be...again. Part of him understood. He had the same affliction—ice-cold feet—when it came to saying I do. But why did Griffin have to get himself in this predicament? Why couldn't he tell a woman on the first date that he wasn't interested in marriage?

"What are you? Chicken?" he asked the three groomsmen.

"Hell, yes," they responded in unison.

"You haven't met the bride." Peter's gaze cut toward the door at the end of the hallway. "She's a knockout, but a...a..."

John combed his fingers through the memory of his hair as if searching for the right description of the bride. "A real pistol."

Eric nodded. "She's something to look at, all right. But I wouldn't want to set her off."

Grant's forehead creased. Maybe that's why Griffin had run back to Dallas like a bull was chasing him.

Squaring his shoulders, Grant prepared to burst the bride's blissful bubble. He would simply handle her the way he dealt with clients whose investments had plummeted on Wall Street. He'd say it straight out. No beating around the bush. If that didn't work then he'd treat her the way he once handled green fillies on his folks' Oklahoma ranch—very carefully. Rotating his neck from side to side, he felt the bow tie tighten its hold on him.

"You'll do fine." John gave a fingertip salute.

"Better than Griffin could." Peter flashed a relieved grin. "He'd probably end up with a black eye or worse."

"You're more diplomatic." Eric rubbed the nape of his neck, as if removing the burden of being the deliverer of bad news. Slowly, he shook his head. "Doesn't seem possible, you and Griffin being brothers. Even though you two look identical, you're like night and day."

"We don't look like each other," Grant growled, but his protest fell on deaf ears.

All of his thirty-five years others had confused him with his twin. And he was damn tired of it. They weren't alike—in looks or deeds. That's why *he'd* settled down in New York, established a career, built something with his life, and Griffin traveled the countryside selling fertilizer, playing footloose and single, then skipping from woman to woman, fiancée to fiancée, wedding to wedding and town to town. Once again, Grant would prove the difference by cleaning up another one of Griffin's messes.

He walked swiftly to the bride's room. No need to postpone the inevitable. Not when there was only half an hour until the wedding was scheduled to begin. The pristine white-painted wooden door, however, put a halt to his determination. The glistening crystal knob unnerved him. He imagined the room decorated for bridal fantasies. Didn't all women daydream about their weddings? Griffin's fiancée probably stood beyond the entrance donning her veil, smiling into a mirror with tears of joy sparkling in her eyes. *God help me.*

He wondered what kind of a woman Annie Baxter was. A real looker? Of course. Griffin wouldn't have agreed to marry someone who looked like a farm animal on one of the nearby ranches. A pistol, eh? Grant rubbed his jaw thoughtfully. Maybe that was the kind of woman his irresponsible brother needed. Griffin liked his women to be seen and not heard. Again, that's where he and his brother differed. Grant preferred a woman with spunk. If he was looking. Which he wasn't. Then he wondered if Annie had a hard right hook.

Cursing under his breath he gave a swift rap on the door and waited until he heard a muffled, "Come on in."

With a deep breath he turned the crystal knob and entered the room. A slight gasp stopped him cold.

An older woman who looked as if she was trying her best to hold back time with a truckload of makeup wagged her finger at him. "You shouldn't be in here." Wearing a hot-pink dress, she looked like a tidal wave of Pepto-Bismol coming toward him. "Don't you know it's bad luck for you to see the bride?"

Hell, the bride's luck couldn't get much worse.

Grant scowled at her. "I need to talk to Annie. Give us a few minutes alone."

"You'll have plenty of time *after* the wedding."

"Thank God." Another voice drew his attention. "You were right, Aunt Maudie. He's here." Excitement lilted the husky voice to a fever pitch.

The bride-*not*-to-be sat on a velveteen chair, her silk-covered legs propped on a table. His gaze traveled up those long, shapely legs to an equally shapely, scantily clad body that had his mouth watering as though he was a teenager gawking at his first centerfold. A lacy garter embraced her hips and thighs like an intimate caress. A matching bra covered her pert breasts. Barely.

*Heaven help me!*

"It's okay." The half-naked bride waved to her aunt. "Give us a few minutes alone." Her seductive drawl had Grant wishing the older woman would stay and chaperone.

With a huff, Aunt Maudie clomped in her high heels around Grant and ducked out the door while muttering, "You're just asking for trouble."

He barely heard the click of the door as it closed behind him. He couldn't concentrate on anything or anyone but Annie.

She lazily swirled a French fry through a ketchup puddle. The hunger in her eyes as she stared at him stirred an automatic, inappropriate response inside him. Slowly, erotically, she tilted back her head and wrapped the French fry around the tip of her tongue. With a half smile, her gaze still holding his, she licked a dollop of ketchup off her bottom lip. With deliberate, self-assured confidence, she uncrossed her legs and stood. He heard the whisper of her stockings as if they were calling to him, inviting him closer.

"I was starving." Her mouth curved into a saucy smile. "Want a bite?"

Grant felt the air sucked out of his lungs. He doubted she was offering her fries. His insides pulled tight with desire and cut off the circulation to his brain. Good God! He was in trouble. He wanted to taste every inch of her delectable body, starting with that tempting swanlike neck, lingering along her curves and planes then working his way down to her petite toes. Trying to shake loose the cloud filling his head with wild ideas, he wondered why Griffin would run hell-bent away from this woman.

She was a pistol all right—with enough gunpowder to blow away a man's good sense. And he felt his senses scattering with each prolonged second.

As she moved, her long legs gliding toward him with a whispering temptation of sex and sin, the only part of her that reminded him of his purpose was the veil crowning her sassy blond tresses. She was his brother's fiancée! Ex-fiancée, he reminded himself.

And he had to break the news to her. Now.

"Annie." He took an unsure step backward trying to cork his steam-heated reaction to her.

He had a job to do. He wished he'd prepared what he was going to say before he'd entered the room. At least then he could recite it and not have to rely on his coherent thoughts, which were no longer so coherent.

"I'm—"

"Oh, Griff! I'm so glad you're here."

Before he could blink, protest or correct her mistake, she wrapped her arms around him and planted a kiss on his mouth. Her lips were warm, moist and open. Irresistible. Stunned, he did what came naturally—he kissed her back.

His nerve endings exploded. Her warm, seductive body aligned with his and tilted his stable world precariously.

*Push her away, you jerk!* he admonished himself. But damn if he could find the strength or the desire. Her hot kiss had somehow debilitated him.

Suddenly, he knew exactly how Griffin had gotten himself backed into this matrimonial corner. Irritated at his own weakness, he placed his hands firmly on her narrow waist and set her away from him. But she locked her arms securely around his neck and drew her leg slowly up along his. Powerful explosions went off in his head and ricocheted through his body, silencing the alarm bells warning him this was a mistake.

She gave a husky sigh that made his insides clench with raw need. He tried to draw a breath, to regain his equilibrium but he failed, miserably.

She started nibbling on his ear and his brain turned to mush. Slanting him a seductive glance, she said, "So, darlin', where are we going on our honeymoon? Which suitcase should I take? The cold- or warm-weather one? Or should we just forget about clothes altogether?"

He swallowed hard.

"Paris? The Swiss Alps? Or did you book a Caribbean cruise?"

*Stop this insanity!*

Her hand inched downward and cupped his backside. He choked and grabbed her wrist. Her tiny bones felt as fragile as winter twigs. Would his news snap her in two? "Annie—"

"I know. You want it to be a surprise." Raising on tiptoe, she nuzzled his neck and sent shock waves along his spine. "Boy, do I have some surprises in store for you!"

*Dammit! I've got a whopper for you, too, lady. Now, get yourself under control, Stevens! She's a woman, just like any other.* But why was telling *this* bride proving to be so much more difficult than the last two?

"I'm anxious for us to be there, for us to finally make love. This waiting is about to kill me." She pressed her breasts against his chest, which somehow suddenly made the room as hot as a Fourth of July firecracker.

His mind spun with the news that his brother had never made love to this bride. Maybe she'd insisted they wait. Maybe that's why Griffin had been so eager to get to the altar.

Gazing up at him, her eyelids drooped lazily...seductively. "Want to start now? The wedding can't start without us."

"Whoa, lady!" Grant cleared his throat, choking on his desire, his deception. "Ah, Annie, I—I'm not who you think I am."

"None of us are." She gave him a smile that scrambled his thoughts like fresh eggs.

How the hell had Griffin ever managed to propose with her gabbing and grabbing? Grant couldn't get a word in edgewise or keep his thoughts straight, much less tell her he wasn't Griffin—and that her groom wasn't coming to the wedding! He moved his hands away from her warm, satiny-smooth waist and up to her shoulders. "Annie—"

"I know what you're thinking," she said in a voice as smooth as warm honey. "This is all so sudden. We didn't date long. We hardly know each other. I think it's sweet that you want to make sure I'm making the right decision." Her hand caressed his jaw. She drew a sensual line from his ear to his chin with her thumb, making his knees as weak as a newborn colt's. "You simply swept me off my feet. What choice did I have but to agree to marry you?"

"Uh..." Disentangling himself from her arms, he stepped away and was finally able to draw a more coherent thought and deeper breath. "I'm Grant." He ran a shaky hand through his hair. "Grant Stevens."

She blinked at him. "What?"

"Griff's..." He shook his head, clearing out the confusion in his own mind. "Griffin's brother."

Her gaze swept over him, narrowing with confusion and disbelief. "Aunt Maudie said...she saw you...that Griff's here." Her hands clenched. "He *is* here."

"No, she must have seen me. You got me confused with Griffin, too."

"But you look just like—"

"We're twins." He bit the words out. "We do not look alike. His eyes are hazel. Mine are gray."

She leaned toward him, resting her hand on his chest as she stood on tiptoe to gaze into his eyes. This time he couldn't avoid her blue hypnotic gaze. "They look the same to me."

Her warm exotic fragrance wrapped around him as seductively and possessively as her arms had earlier.

His gaze was drawn to her parted, moist lips. He tightened his hold on his overblown response to her. An urgent need to prove to her that he was different from his brother rolled over him. "Griffin has freckles across his nose. And I have this scar." He pointed to the bridge of his nose where bride number two had punched him, clipping him with the one-carat diamond Griffin had bought for her with a maxed-out credit card. "See? If you can't tell us apart, then you obviously don't know my brother well enough to marry him."

Her feathery eyebrows slanted down into a frown. She started to touch his scar then their gazes collided. Awareness sparked between them, rekindling the desire deep inside him. She pulled away at the same moment he stepped back. Her eyes widened with dismay. "You kissed me!"

"*You* kissed me," he countered.

"Maybe at first, but I thought you were Griff and I distinctly remember—"

"Griffin's not coming," he cut her off, not wanting his mistake thrown back into his face. He was well aware of the way he'd kissed her. He could still taste her sweetness on his lips, feel her softness and his hardness.

"What? Why?" As quickly as she'd challenged him about the kiss, her expression switched to horror. "What's happened? Is he hurt?"

"Not yet." But when Grant got hold of him...

One of her finely arched eyebrows lifted. "If you're trying to be funny, Gri... Gr..." She gave a slight shake of her head, making the veil caress her bare shoulders. "Uh...Mr. Stevens, it's not working."

"Grant."

"What?"

"My name. It's Grant."

"Where is Griff?"

"I can't say." That didn't sound right so he tried again. "I don't know."

Her shoulders relaxed and she reached for him. "I don't like this practical joke, Griff."

"I'm Grant."

She withdrew as if he'd slapped her.

He gestured toward a nearby blue velveteen chair. "Why don't you have a seat?"

"I don't believe you...any of this." She crossed her arms over her middle, pushing her breasts higher, straining the edges of her lacy bra.

He averted his gaze and tried to remain a gentleman when he'd already failed. "Do you have a...a..."

He spotted a robe flung across the back of a suitcase and retrieved it. He held it out for her to take but she simply stared at him, as if she'd lost all sense.

"Griffin has—" He broke off. The stark pain in her vivid blue eyes reached right into his chest and twisted his heart in a cinch knot. Damn his brother. "Ah, hell, he's backed out of the wedding, Annie. I'm sorry. Sorry he didn't tell you himself." *Sorry he's my lousy brother.*

He watched her carefully, ready to wrap his arms around her if she needed support and just as ready to duck if she threw something at him. Her silence divided his loyalties like a stock split. He searched for something, anything, to say. How could he help her understand? How could he make it easier? Drawing on what she'd told him earlier, he said, "Griffin decided it was too soon...that...uh, you didn't know what you were getting into...marrying him." *Yeah, that's it!* "He was trying to protect you."

Her features contorted and she bent forward.

*Damn, she was going to faint.* He stepped forward. "Annie?"

Her shoulders started to shake.

Wanting to take away the pain she must be feeling, he reached for her, but the sound of her sobs suddenly became clear. She wasn't crying or wailing with anger or grief. She was laughing! Doubled over with laughter!

He jerked his hand back. "What the hell?"

She laughed until her face turned red. At least his tux wouldn't end up damp from a teary bride. Maybe this time he wouldn't land in the emergency room with a broken nose. Or maybe he should call for reinforcements. Maybe she'd gone off the deep end. Feeling as awkward as Jed Clampett visiting Tiffany's he let out a confused chuckle, then gave in to relief.

"So you're not upset?" He sat on the velveteen chair, tension having zapped his strength. "I can't tell you what a relief—"

She took a deep breath then started to choke. Once she had control of herself, she wasn't laughing anymore. "Oh, God. I can't believe this is happening again!"

"......."

# 2

ANGUISH SWELLED inside Annie, but it couldn't get past the sense of hysteria she was feeling. She swallowed the pain and locked it away with the rest she'd endured over the past few years. "This really takes the cake."

Still laughing, not sensing her precarious state of mind, Griffin's brother slapped his knee. "That's a good one. Takes the cake. The wedding cake, right? You've got the right attitude, and a good sense of humor."

Boy, she wished she had the cake with her at the moment. She'd show Griffin. And his twin! She'd dump it first on her fiancé's—ex-fiancé's—head, then she'd...she'd... What?

She wouldn't give in to the tirade that threatened to erupt inside her. She clenched her fists. Not again. She'd made a fool of herself twice before over two men she'd thought she loved. Not this time. Nor would she allow tears to fall. She'd cried enough buckets of tears in the past few years to end the drought here in west Texas. It was time to shut down her emotions and figure out what she would do now.

She grabbed her robe from Grant and with jerky motions shoved her numb arms into the silk sleeves. Somehow with her trembling fingers she managed to tie a knot at her waist.

"I'm glad you're taking this so well," Grant said. "I confess I was worried. Especially the way you kissed me..." This man, this stranger who looked too much like her fiancé for her own comfort and peace of mind, cleared his throat. "The way you kissed me..." He coughed. "I mean...Griffin, uh, earlier. I thought you were really in love."

A heated blush suddenly engulfed her from her toes clear up to her hairline. A rush of blood blocked out his words. *Oh, God! What have I done?*

She wished she could collapse inside her voluminous bridal dress hanging in the corner and disappear. She'd kissed this man, thinking it was her fiancé! And worse, she'd felt her toes curl in a way she'd never experienced before. Not with Griffin, and certainly not with any of her previous fiancés.

She pushed away that nightmare and faced a new one—one that frightened and horrified her more than facing the crowd of expectant family and friends in the chapel. Shouldn't she have realized with that kiss that Grant wasn't her fiancé? Looking back, she realized Grant had made her feel things she'd only wished for with Griff. She bit her lip and refused to contemplate it.

Her head started to pound. She looked at this man claiming to be Griff's brother and searched for some clue she must have missed. He had the same dark brown, almost black, hair that had tiny waves running through it and made her fingers itch to comb it back and tame it...tame him. His eyes did seem similar, yet different. Griffin's had been wild with mischief. This man's were somber, steady, penetrating. Come to think of it, remembering the feel of his body against hers, he had a hard, unrelenting frame, one that could have been an advertisement for any health club, whereas her fiancé's—her *ex*-fiancé's—had been slender and not as well honed.

The backs of her eyes burned as realization settled inside her. She felt her knees go weak. The fact that this man's kiss had made her feel wobbly, more so than any she'd shared with her runaway fiancé, annoyed the heck out of her. "I need to sit down."

Immediately Grant jumped to his feet. "Here."

He helped her into the chair he'd vacated. With one hand on her arm and the other around her waist, she felt a fissure of awareness ripple through her, but it quickly turned to anger. She gazed into her fiancé's face. *No, not Griffin. This is Grant, Griffin's twin.*

Strange how she had the urge to slap his sudden concern right out the door. But she'd save that much effort for when she saw Griff again. *If* she ever saw her ex-fiancé again.

She didn't want Grant's pity or sympathy. She imagined she'd receive enough humiliating helpings of that from family and friends in the next few weeks and months. She cringed remembering how family, friends and busybody neighbors had made her cakes, roast beef and tuna casseroles to show their concern. They'd spoken in funereal tones around her, told her she'd find another man and tried to set her up with any male able to suck in air and stand on two feet. But the whispers behind her back, the knowing, pity-filled glances had told her what they really believed—she was jinxed.

"What do you want me to do?" Grant asked, his

voice soft and soothing in that irritating sympathetic tone she knew all too well.

"Can I get somone? Your bridesmaids?"

Annie shook her head, relieved she hadn't asked any friends to stand by her today. She hadn't wasted any money on useless gowns, either.

"Would water help?" Grant asked.

She stared at him. "Only if I can drown your brother in it."

"I don't blame you for that. In fact, I'd be glad to help. I understand how you feel."

She shook her head. "You can't possibly understand. No one could."

Three's a charm, she thought. Or a curse. How could she have been duped again? She must truly be jinxed when it came to marriage. What was that darn saying? Always the bridesmaid, never the bride? Or maybe she was doomed to always be a bride-to-be, never a full-fledged wife.

That was the story of her life. Her neighbors and friends had probably laid bets to see if this would happen again. She wondered what the odds had been this time.

At least her other two weddings hadn't been canceled at the altar. No, this wedding won that whopping prize. She could shoot Griffin for dumping her this way, for letting her think it was really going to happen, for giving her hope. Why couldn't she have seen it coming? What was wrong with her? Or was it the men she picked?

Neither question soothed her. None of the possible answers quieted her jumbled nerves. Her hands clenched in her lap. Well, by God, she wasn't going to let it happen again! Not in her lifetime.

With renewed spirit, she stood. She was going through with her plans. She was leaving behind the sad memories that had haunted her since her parents' deaths so many years ago and the humiliating ones of her past fiancés. She was going to start over, to see the world. She didn't need a husband or a marriage to do that. She wouldn't stay here and let her life pass her by. No sirree!

But a swift thought took the wind out of her veil. As pathetic and old-fashioned as it sounded, she couldn't leave with folks thinking she couldn't hold on to her man. She stuffed a soggy French fry into her mouth. The salty flavor made it hard to swallow. She wasn't leaving town with her tail—or wedding train—tucked between her legs. Not if she could help it.

"I'm getting married," she spoke the words out loud, surprising herself as much as Grant. "Today."

"You don't seem to understand." He kept his hand firmly on her arm as if she'd lost her grip on reality. "Griffin left. You can't get married without a groom."

She gritted her teeth and shrugged off his hand. "I am getting married."

She'd lived here her whole life. Instead of going off to college, she'd stayed home and commuted to class so she could help her ill mother. She'd wanted to move to a big city to teach, but she'd taken a job at the elementary school she'd attended as a child—all to help her parents.

Then her mother had passed away, leaving her with a last request—that Annie find a good man to marry. She'd tried! Boy, had she tried.

Not long after her mother's death, her father had died of a broken heart. She'd stayed, living in their house, trapped by the fond and sad memories.

Then Rodney came along, swooped her off her feet, made her laugh again. By the time she agreed to marry him, his feet had grown cold. And she'd been left with enormous bills for their wedding that wouldn't be.

Next, Travis strolled into her life. But her second fiancé had a change of heart, this time leaving her with more debt and more reasons to stay in Lockett.

She clenched her hands. "I'm leaving this one-stoplight town if it's the last thing I do."

Grant crossed his arms over his wide chest. "How do you propose to do that?"

"You're going to help me. You offered to help me drown your rotten brother."

"I did. But I was—"

"Don't worry. I'm not planning anything illegal."

"Look, Annie, I regret I had to be the one to tell you, but believe me it's best you found out now how irresponsible Griffin is. He's been like that his whole life. You don't want him."

"You're right. I don't." Her gaze narrowed on him. Then she smiled as her new plan emerged. "I want you."

"What?"

"You're going to marry me…Grant, isn't it?"

He nodded slowly, then shook his head. "Oh, no. I can't help you. I'm not the marrying kind."

"What is this? A family trait? A dominant gene? A birth defect?" She propped her hands on her hips and glared at Grant Stevens. "You're going to marry me. And that's final."

"YOU'RE CRAZY." Stunned, Grant stared at her as if she'd grown an extra head. Had she completely lost touch with reality?

"Possibly." She walked around him, studying him, analyzing him, sizing him up as if he were a prize steer—or maybe not so prized. Not if she saw him being the same as Griffin, the jerk who'd left her at the altar. For some crazy reason, he wanted her to see the differences between him and his irresponsible brother.

"You and Griff really are identical twins. I mean, he told me he had a brother and that y'all were twins, but I assumed you'd only have a familial resemblance. This is truly amazing."

From the fire in her electric-blue eyes, he could tell whatever resemblance he shared with Griffin was not desirable to her at the moment. He'd always hated being compared to his brother. Now he hated it more than ever. "We do not look alike," he ground out between clenched teeth. "Griffin's got a mole on his back, just under his shoulder blade. And I've got—"

Suddenly she grinned, disarming him with that wink of a dimple in her cheek. "This is perfect! Nobody has to know a thing."

"Know what?"

"That you're Grant instead of Griffin." Her forehead creased with concern. "You didn't tell anyone that Griff wasn't coming, did you?"

Relief poured through him. "The groomsmen. So it's too late for whatever it is you're cooking up."

"Drat." Frowning, she paced another minute then stopped, the skirt of her robe giving him a glimpse of a sexy calf. "You can tell them you were wrong. Or better yet, that you were playing a practical joke. Griff loved to play practical jokes."

She spoke of his brother as if he were dead. Maybe in her heart he already was. Grant well remembered his brother's infamous practical jokes. He didn't wait for an excuse like April Fool's. He'd always been the class clown. Grant had been the serious, responsible one.

And that worked well for him now. This woman needed his common sense at the moment. "Annie, there's no way—"

"If there's a will," she said, "then we can make it work. You'll simply pretend you're Griff. We'll get married and be off in our decorated car. Nobody has to know a thing."

Panic seized him. She had lost her grip on reality. "I am not getting married, now or ever."

"You *are* like Griff, aren't you?"

"No, I'm not." His nerves tightened with anger.

He would never promise marriage then walk away from the bride without even a word of explanation. Not that he'd ever asked a woman to marry him. He liked being single. No responsibilities. No honey-do lists. No anniversary or birthday to keep track of. Why would he want to give that up?

The crazy determined light in her eyes looked more dangerous than the curves beneath her silk robe.

"Listen to me, Annie. It's not you."

"Don't tell me it's not personal. This is very personal to me. I'm the one who's been dumped."

"I meant...ah, hell. This is the most ridiculous conversation I've ever had." He hated to be blunt but the circumstances called for it. "You aren't getting married today. I'm sorry. I wish I could make it different. I wish my brother hadn't treated you this way. But you've got to face facts."

"Relax. This isn't for real, forever, or until death do us part. It's just for the afternoon. We'll leave like we're going on our honeymoon and that will be the end of it. You can drop me at the airport and then you never have to see me again."

"But—"

She grabbed his arm, her fingers crumpling the sleeve of his tuxedo with desperation. "Please."

The plea in her voice and gaze knocked him for a loop. How could he say no?

But he had to. It was the right thing to do. "You don't know what you're saying. Maybe I should call a doctor. You've had quite a shock."

"I'm perfectly rational. This makes sense. It will work."

"It's not right. What about all those people out there? You're going to lie to your family and friends?"

She worried her bottom lip. "It's not exactly lying. Think of it as a practical joke. They'll just never know the punch line."

"I don't do practical jokes."

She pursed her lips. "You've got to help me." Tears made her eyes sparkle like sapphires. "If it wasn't for your brother I wouldn't be in this predicament."

Oh, God! Not tears. Anything but tears.

Then an alarming question popped into his mind.

"Are you pregnant?" Maybe she'd slept with his brother after all.

Her eyes widened. "No. It's nothing like that. I—I can't..." her voice wavered "...face them."

"You won't have to. I'll handle everything. I'll make the announcement. It's the least I can do."

She blinked and those tears disappeared. Her jaw hardened. "I live here. I can't listen to remarks about poor, pitiful Annie. I refuse to be a jilted bride again."

Her words punched him like a jab in the solar plexus. His jaw went slack before he recovered. "Again?" His hands clenched into fists. "Griffin's done this to you before?"

She frowned and pulled away from him. As she paced the length of the room, her silk robe rustling, he remembered distinctly what she was wearing—or wasn't wearing—beneath. *Don't lose focus. Concentrate. You can't give in to her crazy idea. Or your libido.*

"This isn't the first time this has happened," she told him. "Okay, it's the first wedding-day disaster. But Griff's not the first man to dump me. The other two left days before the big date. I never got this close to walking down the aisle." To herself, she spoke softly. "Maybe everybody was right. Maybe I am jinxed."

Then she swung around and faced him. He caught another brain-fogging glimpse of long, silky legs. But it was the pure intensity and determination in her bright blue eyes that melted his reservations. He didn't pity her. In fact, he knew she'd bounce back from this disaster. He admired her buoyancy.

"I can't face them as a deserted bride again. Please." She took a step forward and touched his chest, reminding him of the barely suppressed intimacy they'd shared in that sizzling kiss. "Please, Grant, help me. This once."

Damn. What else could he do? Damn Griffin. Damn himself for wanting to help.

"Okay," he finally said. "I'll play along. Just for today. Then the charade will be over and we'll go our separate ways."

And he'd make Griffin pay for this. Next time his brother could clean up his own mess...and marry his own fiancée.

Annie's face transformed into a dazzling smile. Before he could brace himself, she hugged him close, her body colliding with his, her curves reminding him of the dangers of her body, her kiss. His pulse jolted into high gear. Her musky scent whispered to him like a lover's invitation. Her blue eyes beckoned to him. He felt the definite tug of desire. His gaze dropped to her mouth and he remembered how sweet and tempting she tasted.

"Thank you," she whispered before he could dip his head for another forbidden sample. "You won't regret this."

But he already did.

THE WEDDING BELLS RANG through the chapel, chiming the hour, then the organist began the march. The chords roared in Annie's head and jangled her nerves. She felt as if she'd buckled in her emotions for a wild roller-coaster ride and wasn't exactly sure they'd stay in their seats. Her veil made everything seem blurry and surreal. It pressed in on her, imprisoning her in a shroud of lies.

She had imagined tears of joy as she walked down the aisle, not tears of frustration and defeat. She refused to give in to the threatening sobs choking her. This was supposed to be her wedding day, the happiest day of her life. Not the worst.

Feeling her mouth tremble, she squared her shoulders, lifted her chin and took the first step down a long white carpeted walkway. She felt as if she was walking through quicksand, each step taking every ounce of energy she possessed. She walked down the aisle toward her fake groom, who looked way too much like Griffin for her peace of mind.

She kept her eyes trained on Grant and tried to look on the bright side—if there was one. At least Griffin had a twin who could save her from total humiliation.

There was a wildness about Grant, not a silly funny bone like Griff, but an untamed side that intrigued her. He looked tall, dark and sexy in his tux, the quintessential groom, a definite prize. The stark white collar accentuated his sun-bronzed features. The ebony jacket showed off his broad-as-Texas shoulders and slim waist. She'd switched his pale pink rosebud boutonniere for the white one reserved for the groom. Somehow his metallic gaze pulled her toward him, steadied her, gave her confidence.

She should have been reminded of her ex-fiancé when she looked at him, but now she could see the subtle differences in the two men. Grant's eyes were a silvery-gray, compassionate yet hard-edged. His features were tanned, making the tiny white scar on the bridge of his nose stand out. And his body...well, she remembered the hard feel of him against her, his hands at her waist, his mouth on hers. She felt a surge of heat from her satin-covered toes to her veil.

*Annie! You shouldn't be having thoughts like that—at a time like this.*

Feeling self-conscious and uncomfortable playing the part of a bride, she refused to look at the smiling, curious and surprised faces of family and friends sitting along the wooden pews. She figured most had simply come to see if the twice-dumped bride would finally get to say "I do," or to see what catastrophe would keep the wedding from taking place. If only they knew!

Her jaw clenched. They wouldn't know. Not if she could help it. And Grant Stevens better not slip up and let the cat out of the proverbial bag. *Damn Griff! The least he could have done was tell her himself.*

Actually, she wouldn't have taken that well, either. But at least then she could have pretended the decision was hers. That *she'd* dumped *him!* Oh, how she would like to drop-kick him all the way to Dallas.

Her hand tightened around the cascading bouquet of white roses, Casablanca lilies and stephanotis blooms. Once again, she felt the sharp bee sting of rejection. A burning ache resonated outward from her heart and throbbed in her veins. *Why, oh why, had this happened again?*

Grant gave her a cautious, if not worried, smile. He held out his arm for her and she put her hand in the crook. Suddenly she felt safe. It was an odd time to feel that way as she stood at the front of the chapel about to take false vows with a stranger, knowing it was a big lie to her family and friends. Still a calm settled over her.

She'd never been able to lie. Never fibbed. How could anyone get away with something like that in a small town anyway? Someone always tattled or gossiped.

But not this time. There'd be no one here to reveal her secret once she'd left with a handsome groom on her arm and her hopes and dreams packed in her suitcases. For the first time in the past seven years, she felt relieved that her parents weren't alive to see this farce, this fiasco!

She'd always tried to do the right thing, always been the Goody Two-shoes, always toed the line. What had she done to deserve this? Well, she wasn't going to sit back and take what life handed out anymore. This time she was taking her life in her own hands, making her own way, pushing the limits. And boy was she pushing the boundaries today.

This time she wasn't a poor, defenseless victim, a romantic sap who'd fallen in love with the wrong man—again. This was her way out of a humdrum life stuck in a nothing-happening town. By this evening, she'd be on her own...free.

Heck, she decided suddenly, it was better than getting married. Why, she could do anything her heart desired. Freedom would be fulfilling, exciting, an adventure. She could go anywhere, do anything. And she would.

The only thing she wouldn't be getting was a lovely romantic, sexy honeymoon.

She felt Grant's muscles shift and tighten beneath the fine cloth. He seemed as steady and solid as a rock, where Griff had been slender as a reed, obviously bending and swaying to his own whims. When she thought of her ex-fiancé, anger swirled inside her. So she kept her focus on Grant, on the way his gaze warmed her, on his generous mouth, on the memory of his kiss.

Just the recollection had her insides twitching with need. Her skin burned as she remembered all she'd said to him, even though she hadn't known he wasn't her fiancé.

But he had! Still he hadn't stopped the kiss. He'd deepened it, held her intimately against him. She couldn't be mistaken about that. But why?

It didn't matter. It didn't matter at all. He was her *temporary* groom. End of story—or so it would be when he dropped her at the airport.

"Annie," he whispered.

Her gaze lifted to his, and she saw concern darkening his eyes to a deep, somber gray. "Huh?"

He gave a nod toward the preacher.

"Oh, uh, I do."

The man who'd married her parents, baptized her as a child and eulogized her parents at their funerals gave a slight shake of his head. Reverend Sarks offered her a sympathetic smile as a murmur of laughter rippled through the congregation. Embarrassment burned inside her. What had she done now?

"Let me repeat," the preacher said, "and then you copy what I say, Annie. Okay?"

She gave a slight nod of understanding. *Pay attention or you'll blow this.*

"I, Annie Meredith Baxter," she repeated Reverend Sarks's words, her throat tight, her heart pounding, "take this man, Gra...uh, Griffin Thomas Stevens, to be my lawfully wedded husband."

Reluctantly she felt her gaze drawn back to Grant. What kind of husband would he make? Was he really as different from Griff as he declared?

*It doesn't matter, Annie! Good grief, you're not marrying him anyway.* Distinctly she remembered that his aversion to marriage matched his brother's. And now she shared that same aversion.

"To have and to hold from this day forward." She waited for Reverend Sarks's next cue. "For better or worse." *Couldn't get much worse than today.* "For richer for poorer. In sickness and health." *If I ever run into Griff, he's dead meat.*

She'd tried the marriage route three times now and that was enough. From now on, she was on her own. She didn't need a man. Not even one as devastatingly handsome as Grant Stevens.

It disturbed her that she wasn't more upset about Griff's desertion. Anger dominated her feelings more than grief. Her one regret was that she wouldn't be leaving today on a romantic honeymoon. Maybe she was in shock.

Dangerously, her mind skipped back to that kiss she'd shared with Grant. Her tongue tripped over itself and she flubbed the last words of her vows, "Till kiss us do part."

Her gaze flew to Grant and a flame flared deep inside her. Laughter sifted through the congregation.

"Till death, darlin'," Grant said, his mouth pulling to the side in a semblance of humor. "Our kiss is just the beginning."

His words gripped her heart. If only!

No, no. She didn't want Grant or his brother or any other man. She'd do just fine on her own. After today, that is. She'd be grateful to Grant for his help and support through this difficult day, but gratitude was where it would end. And the upcoming kiss would be their last.

"Right, padre?" Grant slanted his gaze toward Reverend Sarks.

"It's nice to see such an eager groom." He gave an official nod. "By the power vested in me by the state of Texas I pronounce you husband and wife. Kiss your bride."

Annie should have been prepared. She should have been numb with shock and grief or trembling with anger. But when Grant lifted her veil and looked at her with that mercurial gaze, she felt her temperature rising.

# 3

NEVER IN HIS WILDEST imaginings had Grant ever thought he'd utter the words *I do*. He prided himself on being the practical brother, the responsible one. Why did this seem like the dumbest mistake he'd ever made? This was something Griffin would do. And Grant would have been the one to sit back, shake his head and laugh at his younger-by-two-minutes twin.

His mind tripped over the phrase "Kiss your bride." She wasn't his. And he certainly didn't want a bride. But hell, what was he supposed to do? Ignore the time-honored tradition? He *had* to kiss her.

Remembering all too well the passion her first kiss had fired inside him, he made a conscious decision to make this kiss brief and chaste. There wasn't a rule book on wedding kisses that said it had to be deeply intimate or even very long. Any old kiss would do. Wouldn't it?

Cupping her jaw, feeling her tremble beneath his touch, he wondered what she was thinking. Was she remembering their first kiss, too? Or was she wishing he was Griffin? And that she was truly married?

He felt awkward as a schoolboy about to kiss his first girl. But this time he had an audience. What did they expect? Something tender and sweet? Bells and whistles? Firecrackers?

Then he remembered that Annie wanted to impress

the socks off her hometown crowd. She wanted them
to think she was good and married, forever and ever,
amen. All thoughts of a chaste kiss evaporated.

His gaze shifted toward Annie's pink mouth. He
noticed the generous curve along the bottom lip, the
bowlike shape of the top, and his focus narrowed,
blocking out the chapel full of witnesses, erasing
every thought but one: He *wanted* to kiss Annie again.

That frightening thought made a bead of sweat
trickle down his spine. Ignoring the pounding of his
heart and the warning bells in his head, he leaned forward, took her shoulders between his hands and
slanted his mouth across hers. He felt her melt into
him, her bones turning pliable, her back arching toward him. He deepened the kiss, tasted her warmth,
her passion. Something inside him shifted, a powerful
need gripped him.

What the hell was he doing?

And what was Annie doing? Just making a show?
Or was she believing this? Was she loco? Did she believe they were really and truly married?

Panic arced through him and he pulled away. A
roar sounded in his ears. He tried to give himself a
mental shake to clear the cobwebs she'd caused. Then
he realized the crowd behind them was cheering.

"Hey, Griffin!" Eric—who'd stepped in to be the
best man when Grant had told the groomsmen it had
all been a practical joke and that his twin from New
York had missed his flight—clapped him on the back.
"Save your energy for the honeymoon."

Grant cringed at being called his brother's name but
swallowed his irritation and tried to look like the ex-
uberant bridegroom.

John, the next groomsman in line, gave a sheepish grin. "You're gonna need it."

"Sure did fool us before the wedding, pretending to be your brother and calling off the wedding," Peter, the last groomsman, mumbled and slanted his gaze toward Annie. "Who wouldn't want to go on a honeymoon with that babe?"

Grant's spine stiffened. "Are you referring to my wife?"

"Uh, yeah, uh, I mean...what isn't there to love about Annie?"

"That's better." Satisfied, Grant wrapped his arm around Annie's waist. Why did he feel so protective of this woman? Maybe because his brother had treated her like a bad blind date.

By the time all the pictures were taken, Grant had a headache from the camera flashes. It had to be the lights, not that Annie's hand was linked with his and her warm body pressed against his side.

"This way, Griffin!" Eric called, leading the wedding party to the reception. "Make way, folks, for the bride and groom."

Being called his brother's name made Grant's cummerbund feel constricting. Instead of gritting his teeth and giving his usual response that he wasn't his brother, he let it pass and managed a tight smile.

The rest of the afternoon passed in a blur of repetitious words of congratulations. Had everyone in this entire town turned out for the event? The receiving line looked long enough to wrap around a city block. He told himself that putting up with the charade was the least he could do for Annie and promised himself Griffin would suffer someday soon.

Sticking out his hand, he greeted the next guest. "Thanks for coming."

The man pumped Grant's hand like an oil rig. "Good to know you. Henry Norton. Grew up here with Annie's papa. Smoked a cigar with Ralph Baxter—God rest his soul—the day she was born."

Grant smiled at the image of Annie's father celebrating the birth of his daughter. He wondered what she'd looked like as a baby, if there'd been even a hint of the beauty that he saw now. "Grant Ste—"

Annie dug her fingers into his arm.

He froze. Good God! What had he done?

Then Annie laughed. "Oh, Griff! What a card you are. But you're starting to bore us with that old joke, pretending to be your twin brother."

"Old habit," he managed to say.

The older gentleman eyed him carefully then gave a quick nod and moved on down the line.

By the time they'd cut the cake, Annie's smile had congealed. He kept close to her side, hoping she'd point out anyone in the throng of guests that he was supposed to know so she'd cover any of his gaffes. After a while, he realized Griffin had been a phantom fiancé. Most folks here thought Annie had just made him up out of thin air.

If only they knew the truth!

"Well, sugar—" the Pepto-Bismol lady approached and embraced Annie "—you're a married woman. Your mama can rest in her grave now."

Grant noticed a tear well at the corner of Annie's eye but she blinked it away. He reached for her hand and gave a gentle squeeze. Annie met his gaze, and her mouth curved in a tremulous smile. His chest tightened with a strange set of emotions that he couldn't decipher.

"And you, young fellow!" The bleached blonde snapped her arms around him like a banker's clip. "Don't let word get back to Annie's aunt Maudie that you done her wrong. You hear?"

"Yes, ma'am."

Ending her hug with a loud clap to his back, she gave him a jab in the ribs with her elbow and looped arms with the bride and groom. "Now, let me give y'all the recipe for honeymoon salad."

"Aunt Maudie..." Annie began.

"Listen up, sugar. I should know about these things. I've been married almost more times than there are days of the week. For the perfect honeymoon salad, there's no dressing required." She tipped back her head and roared with laughter.

Annie's cheeks turned a bright pink that matched her aunt's dress. Grant felt a cord of desire yank tight inside him. Too bad there wouldn't be a honeymoon for Annie and him.

What the hell was he thinking?

"Here comes the champagne," Aunt Maudie announced. "And not too soon."

First she handed a flute to both the bride and groom then reached for her own. Tapping a gaudy ring on the crystal, she gained the attention of the crowd that circled them like eager vultures. Grant wondered what they'd do if they knew the truth, if they learned that his brother had stood Annie up and that he himself would be dumping her at the airport. Would they tar and feather him and ride him out of town on a rail?

From the look of a group of ranchers eyeing him closely, he wouldn't put it past them.

"I'd like to make a toast," Aunt Maudie said, lifting her voice above the din. "To my beautiful niece. May you two live and love like there is no tomorrow. And may the smile that starts on your wedding night never fade."

Looping his arm around Annie's, Grant gulped down his embarrassment and tasted the champagne. His bride leaned forward and put her mouth along the lip of the flute and tasted the fruity, bubbly wine. He couldn't seem to drag his gaze away. He remembered her kisses and wanted more. Hell, she was more intoxicating than the wine.

Dipping his head, he couldn't resist the temptation to kiss her once more. This time the kiss was brief. But the impact was as powerful as the others.

She smiled at him...or at Griffin. Damn!

Who did he see when she looked at him? It grated on his nerves that this beautiful woman, who was holding his hand and sharing champagne kisses with him, loved his brother. What had she seen in his twin?

This crazy wedding was getting to him, too. Maybe there was something in the water...or champagne. What was wrong with him? Annie was not *his* bride, not even a potential date. Hell, she should have been his sister-in-law. And that would have been a damn shame.

For one insane moment, he wished her smiles and kisses were for him. That was his most dangerous thought yet.

He disentangled himself from her and took a step away. He still couldn't draw a full breath though.

What was in that champagne? Or was it Annie's kisses that had drugged him?

Whatever it was, he knew he needed to get away from her. And fast!

BENEATH A CASCADE of rose petals, they raced toward the decorated car parked in front of the church. The velvety aroma embraced Annie just as Grant's solid arm held her firmly against his side. She caught a glimpse of a few suggestive sayings shoe-polished onto the car windows along with a string of balloons attached to the side mirrors. She gave a self-satisfied smile. The wedding and reception couldn't have gone better—except if she'd actually gotten married.

But she wouldn't—couldn't—think of that now. Even a sexy fake groom was better than none, especially when her old school chums and fellow teachers had drooled all over Grant.

Grant...not Griffin. She figured her ex-fiancé, if he'd shown up for their wedding, would have charmed them the way he'd dazzled her with slick talk and Casanova grins—but not with the same sincerity and savoir faire Grant seemed to possess. A peculiar feeling tightened her stomach. This charade was about to end.

Then she wouldn't have Grant's strong shoulder to lean against, his warm smile encouraging her or his kisses tempting her to forget her recent heartache. Why that should bother her, she wasn't sure. She certainly didn't want to analyze the reasons.

With her friends and family cheering and engulfing the car, Grant held the door open for her. Bunching her skirt around her, she slid into the passenger seat, but her train and veil trailed out the door. Grant gathered the material and settled it across her legs. His hand brushed her calf, making her skin tingle and sending tiny electric sparks along her spine.

But he didn't seem to notice his effect on her. He didn't pause or meet her startled gaze. He slammed the door closed and darted around the car.

Well, why should he notice anything? He wasn't her groom. He was supposed to have been her brother-in-law. But why did he make her feel things she shouldn't be feeling with a stranger on her wedding day?

Simple. He looked too much like her fiancé, almost making her forget he wasn't Griffin. Almost, but not quite. That in itself was a risky acknowledgment.

Grant had a different type of charisma, a quiet charm that unsettled her. Griffin had been boisterous and entertaining, but he'd never made her feel emotionally vulnerable. And that had given her a false sense of security, she realized now, looking back. But Grant made her feel as if she was on the verge of something, teetering on the edge of a cliff. He had a way of looking at her that made her feel exposed, as if he could see through her defenses right into her soul. His touch ignited her. And his kisses! Oh, Lord, she didn't need to think about his kisses.

Maybe it was best if they parted ways—and soon.

"We're off," Grant said, gunning the engine of his rental car. The sedan took off with a jolt and peeled out of the parking lot.

Annie resisted the temptation to look back, to second-guess her decision to leave her hometown. This was for the best. She'd said her goodbyes. Now it was time to move on to her new life. Still, she felt a tiny catch of sadness mixed with remorse in her chest.

Being alone for the past few years had been difficult enough in a small town where she knew her neighbors as well as she knew herself. She'd missed her parents. Their deaths had shaken her to the core, left her all alone without anyone but Aunt Maudie to call family. Living in her parents' house had only made her pain and isolation more acute. But being all alone in a big city suddenly seemed more bleak. She'd be truly alone, with no one to turn to for comfort or even a shared memory.

Her stomach rolled, waves of doubt crashing through her. What if she was making another mistake? If she was, then at least she'd suffer the consequences anonymously. No one would ever have to know. Besides, it was already too late. She'd already burned the proverbial bridge to her hometown. There was no going back now—not unless she wanted to confess her wedding had been a charade. And be the laughingstock of Lockett? No way!

A clanking noise startled her. Oh, great. Just what they needed—car trouble. Would this interfere with their clean getaway?

"What's that?" she asked, glancing over her shoulder.

"Cans," Grant answered, looking calm and collected. "The groomsmen tied them onto the bumper."

"Oh." She slumped back into her seat, exhaustion from the long, traumatic day settling into her bones. "They really went all out, what with shoe polish and balloons."

He cleared his throat. "Uh-huh," he said, smirking.

Annie glanced at him. "What's wrong?"

"Nothing." He seemed to stop fighting it and broke into a grin.

She felt her insides dissolve like ice cream in July. But it couldn't be his dazzling smile, she reasoned. It had to be the summer sun beating down on them. "Tell me."

He shot her a glance. "Are you that innocent?"

"What?" Confused, she tried to figure out what piece of the conversation she'd missed. "What do you mean?"

He rubbed his jaw. "You and Griffin didn't..."

"Didn't what?" Drained of patience, she heard the defensiveness in her own voice. "What are you talking about?"

"Never mind. It's none of my business." He cast a glance toward the balloons flapping and turning in the wind. "Those aren't balloons, Annie."

She leaned toward him, squinting to look out his window. The balloons weren't a normal shape for the helium-filled variety. The color was a neutral shade not a vibrant color, as you'd expect to see at a circus. Realization dawned. She felt her hairline burn with embarrassment. "Oh my."

That's why he'd thought she was an innocent! She hadn't recognized—hadn't even thought about—the balloons being condoms. Worse than that, he knew she and Griffin hadn't had sex. Why that should be so awful she wasn't sure. But it was.

Did he think she was a virgin? That she couldn't satisfy her man? That Griff had gotten cold feet because she'd given him a cold shoulder in bed? She jerked her chin. It didn't matter what Grant thought.

Still, her skin blazed. She tried to remember back to what else she'd said to him when they'd first met, when she'd believed he was Griff, when she'd practically thrown herself at him. Her head pounded. She didn't want to think about that.

"Don't worry," he said, his tone a mixture of reassurance and good humor. "I'm sure they'll pop or something before we get to the airport."

"Right. The airport." Where they'd say goodbye.

Why did that thought disconcert her? Probably because she'd depended on Grant all day. And he'd actually come through for her, shown her he was dependable, whereas other men—especially her fiancés—had proven the opposite. When they reached the airport, she'd be on her own. For good.

But that was fine with her, she assured herself. She wanted freedom, not some man.

Grant reached toward the rearview mirror and adjusted it. She noticed his strong, tanned hands and remembered the feel of them touching her waist, grasping her hand, caressing her face just before he'd kissed her at the altar. Something stirred inside her. Irritated, she worked on straightening out her veil, smoothing out the wrinkles.

How she wished she'd changed into something else before heading to the airport. But a few days ago Griff had told her he wanted to show off his bride to all the world. Also, he'd said they wouldn't have time before their flight. Maybe he'd simply wanted to humiliate her even more.

Feeling her body tense with questions that she'd probably never know the answers to, she needed something to take her mind off Griff. "So—" she focused on Grant "—I didn't get much of a chance to talk to you before the wedding. You live in New York. Is that right?"

"Year-round."

"The Big Apple!" She felt a surge of energy. "How long have you lived there?"

"Ten years."

She gave a dreamy sigh and leaned her head back, imagining the vital hum of the city, the excitement, the millions of places to eat. "Someday I'm going there. I don't know how or when. But someday... And I'm going to Paris, Naples, Rome, Edinburgh..." Slanting her gaze toward him, she said, "What do you do in New York?" She brazenly gave him a once-over. "You don't sell manure like your brother, do you?"

He laughed. "There aren't too many ranches or farms in The City."

"The City," she repeated. "I like that. Sounds like it's the only one that matters."

His mouth quirked with the semblance of a smile, then disappeared. "I'm an investment banker."

"On Wall Street?"

"The one and only."

"You must love living there."

"You get used to it."

Curious, she tilted her head and studied him, wondering what exactly he meant. "Sounds like an exciting place. So much to see and do. Nothing happens in small towns."

"I wouldn't say nothing." He shot her a pointed look. "Or maybe I'm wrong. How many fake weddings happen in Lockett every day?"

She gave a wry smile. "Not that many. But thanks to you we pulled it off. What can I do to repay you?"

"No need. I'd say we're even, after what my brother—" He cut himself off. "Sorry, Annie. If you want, I'll beat Griffin up the next time I see him."

From the way his hands gripped the steering wheel, she knew he would and could truly make Griffin regret what he'd done. But she wasn't looking for revenge; she simply wanted her own life. If only she'd realized that before making a mistake and accepting Griff's proposal.

Moved by Grant's willingness to stand up for her, defend her, she touched his hand. The titillating effect made her rethink making contact with him. Folding her hands in her lap, she watched him maneuver the car around a truck hauling hay bales. He was self-assured, confident, but not reckless—not like Griffin.

"I'm okay," she said, feeling stronger than she had a few short hours ago when she'd learned Griff had skipped town. "Really. I've been through this before. Not quite as dramatic as today, but I'll survive."

"I'm sure you will." Again he checked the rearview mirror. "Most of the folks at the wedding...were they friends and family members of yours?"

"Mostly friends and neighbors. It was a long way for Griffin's friends to travel on such short notice."

"Yeah, well, they probably weren't too sure it would happen. I know I had my doubts. But I wasn't willing to risk missing my brother's wedding. Most of your guests," he said, changing topics abruptly, "they, uh, must be from around these parts."

"Well, yeah. Sure. Most live in town. That's where I was raised."

He frowned at the rearview mirror. "Were they planning a party after the wedding?"

Confused, she studied him for a moment. "Not that I'm aware of."

"Wouldn't be going to Amarillo to kick up their heels, would they?"

"Why?" she asked.

"Because we seem to be leading a tailgate party."

Pushing her veil and skirt out of the way, Annie swiveled as best she could in her seat. "Oh, no!" She recognized several of the cars following at a discreet distance. "Great. I bet they're going to give me a send-off at the airport. Can you lose them?"

"I'm driving the speed limit."

"But this is an emergency!"

"Wouldn't they know we're going to the airport and get there anyway?"

She slumped back in her seat. Her stomach sunk with despair. "You're right." Panic started to set in, making her nerves jangle together. "What are we going to do?"

"How about tell the truth? We could explain what happened. I'm sure they'd understand."

"Absolutely not!" She'd be humiliated—more than she had been already. "We've come this far. We've got to figure something out." She clutched his arm, making the car swerve until he regained control. "You've got to help me."

# 4

HORNS BLARED.

"What the hell do they want?" Grant asked. "For us to pull over?"

Annie looked over her shoulder, and Grant followed her gaze in the rearview mirror. The wedding convoy trailed his rental car like the coffee cans the groomsmen had attached to the bumper that had fallen off several miles back.

"They're cheering us on," she said, surprise and humor making her voice lilt.

She sidled closer to him and slid her arm around his shoulders, leaned more heavily against him. He could feel the curve of her breast against his arm. A jolt of awareness shot through him. He should move away, but he couldn't. He was trapped. And half the town of Lockett was behind them, watching!

"Remember," she said, her voice a husky whisper in his ear, as if those in the cars following them might overhear, "they think we're a loving couple on the way to our honeymoon."

"Only until we get to the airport," he said. "Then we'll have to tell them the truth."

She stiffened before pulling away. "You won't help me, then?"

He refused to peer into those vibrant blue eyes again. It would only get him into trouble. Pretending to be his brother for a day, plus getting married—even just for show—had been more than enough for Grant. It was time to end this charade.

"There's nothing we can do, Annie. The jig is up."

"Not yet." She drummed her fingers against the armrest and he knew she was concocting a new plan.

"I'll explain it to them," he offered in a supportive, positive tone.

She had to be sensible about this. Before they dug themselves in deeper than they already had. Before she got the crazy idea they had to produce kids. Before she insisted he go to her high-school reunion in ten years. Before it was time to celebrate their pretend fiftieth anniversary. This had to end sometime. Now was as good a time as any.

"They're your friends and family," he said. "They'll understand. They'll support you."

"No."

"They won't?"

"I can't leave as a jilted bride. If Griff had been the first, then maybe. But he's the third!" Her voice lifted to an hysterical pitch. "They have to believe I'm married."

"But why?"

She crossed her arms over her chest, giving him a look that made him feel like all this was his fault anyway. Guilt by association. The groom-not-to-be was his brother. "You can't possibly understand."

"Try me."

"Look, Grant..." The way she said his name had him wanting to duck for cover. "We can figure this out. Together, we can think of something."

"What?"

"I don't know."

He knew he wouldn't be able to say no to whatever her next scheme would be. Damn.

"Maybe we can distract them," she said. "I can buy a ticket...for somewhere...anywhere. You can hop your plane back to New York, and they'll think we're off on our honeymoon, doing all the things honeymooners are supposed to do."

Grant gripped the steering wheel hard. He remembered her hungry kiss, the curves of her body pressed against him, eager, yearning. Heat flashed through his body. He couldn't think of honeymoons. He sure shouldn't be thinking of Annie on a honeymoon. "Don't you have plane tickets that Griff bought?"

"Like I'd go on my honeymoon alone!" Her chin jutted out. "Besides, Griff has them. He's probably headed to Paris right now." She grabbed his arm, forcing him to look at her. "You don't think he took someone else, do you?"

*Yes.*

"No," he said instead.

Unfortunately Grant knew his brother too well to believe what he wanted Annie to believe. No reason for her to be hurt any more than she already was.

So he added more. "Of course not. He wouldn't do that."

She tapped her fingers against her lips as if debating with herself if she should ask more questions or not. He couldn't quite forget the shape or texture or taste of her lips.

"I hope you're right," she said.

It didn't matter if he was or not. She'd never see Griffin again. And in a few minutes she'd say goodbye to Grant. He didn't know why he felt a mixture of regret and relief.

"Look!" Annie leaned toward the windshield, her face brightening. She was staring at the red D-Q sign just up ahead. "Have you ever had one of their parfaits?"

"Can't say that I have."

"Would you mind pulling through the drive-thru so I can get one?"

His eyes slanted toward the rearview mirror and the line of cars trailing them. "But—"

"Please. It may be a while before I return." She settled back into the cushion of her seat, her dress forming a cloud around her.

He clicked on his turn signal and mumbled, "Why do I think I'm going to regret this?"

NOTHING HAD HAPPENED at the fast-food joint. The tailgaters had kept a respectful distance. But Grant sensed their luck was changing now that they'd arrived at the airport. He figured they were in for a big sendoff. Trouble was, the "honeymooners" weren't going anywhere. And his flight was scheduled for takeoff a little after four.

He kept an eye on the luggage as Annie zipped into the bathroom to try to rub out the dab of chocolate she'd dropped on the full skirt of her wedding dress. He saw *them* first and ducked behind a kiosk selling magazines, chewing gum and breath mints.

"Where'd they go?" one of them, a man in a blue suit, asked no one in particular. His gaze darted and shifted like a New York pedestrian trying to cross a cab-clogged Thirty-fourth Street.

"How could we have lost them? They look like they belong on top of a wedding cake!" A blonde dressed in an obnoxious shade of pink rushed up beside the man. "Do you know what time their flight was?"

"I don't even know where they're going. Do you?"

The blonde shook her head and shifted to the side as another friend or neighbor or relative of Annie's barreled through the revolving door. "Are they here?"

"We don't know yet."

The round woman that looked like a big serving of vanilla ice cream propped her hands on her hips. "Well, they've gotta be around here somewhere."

Grant grabbed a magazine and watched them from behind the pages of *Good Housekeeping*. All three of them scanned the area, their gazes like shotgun pellets exploding around the airport.

"Can you believe she finally did it?" The round woman fanned herself as if she'd run all the way to the airport from Lockett.

"No," the pink-parfait woman said. "I never thought she'd hook one."

The man nodded solemnly like a minister presiding over a funeral. He straightened his striped tie. "I thought this groom would run out on her, too."

Grant clenched his hands, crinkling the magazine's pages. Why did her so-called friends think her latest groom would dump her? There was nothing wrong with Annie. In fact, he'd been surprised to learn Griffin was the third. He would have thought just by her looks she'd have potential grooms lined up around the block.

"Did you see the way her groom looked at her?" the

blonde asked, rolling her eyes as if she'd just sampled a rich torte.

"He must really be in love with her."

"Never thought I'd see it happen."

"How come?"

The man rubbed his jaw. "Annie's just...too much. Maybe she'll fit into a big city better than Lockett. Where'd she say her groom lives? Dallas? Houston?"

The women shrugged.

"We sure will miss her though," one said.

"Yeah," the other woman said. "Who will we have to gossip about now? Nobody pulls the stunts that Annie does."

Grant clenched his teeth and swallowed the words that jammed his throat. What kind of friends, neighbors, relatives were these? No wonder Annie had said they wouldn't understand her predicament or her reason for pretending to get married instead of admitting Griffin had pulled an inexcusable stunt.

Squaring his shoulders, Grant realized Annie was right. She had to leave Hickville, married. And the sooner the better.

The broad woman sighed. "But she sure did get herself a looker."

"Mm-mmm." The pink lady fanned her face with her hand. "I wish I'd seen him first. I would have given Annie a run for her money."

Grant had heard enough. He replaced the magazine on the rack and backed slowly around the kiosk. Making his way to the ticket counter, he made a rash decision. And he knew he would regret it later. But not now. For now, he couldn't see straight for the anger boiling inside him.

"Can I help you?" the airline employee asked with a guaranteed smile.

"I need another ticket for the 4:05 to New York."

"I'LL PAY YOU BACK," Annie said. "I promise."

"Don't worry about it." It was the least he could do. After all, it was his brother who'd dumped her, who'd put her in this situation. That's right. It was only obligation and sibling guilt that had made him whisk her off to New York with him.

"So, I guess you don't do this every day?"

"What? Fly?"

"No. Get married. Save a jilted bride."

"Well, actually..."

"You have? Really? Who?"

"I haven't gotten married before, for real or otherwise," he said.

"So I was your first, eh?" She winked, making his pulse race. "Was it good for you?"

Suddenly the plane felt too damn warm. He jerked loose his bow tie and signaled the flight attendant.

"Yes, sir?" The flight attendant, who was as tall and thin as a swizzle stick, leaned against the seat in front of him.

"Could I have a drink?"

"Not before takeoff, sir." Then she smiled. "Did you two just get married?"

"No, we just like to run around in these getups." He regretted his sarcasm.

The flight attendant's smile never wavered. "Long day, huh?"

"You can't begin to imagine," Annie said.

"The longest," Grant agreed.

"I got married three months ago," the flight attendant said. "Between my in-laws and siblings squabbling over stuff, I wish we'd eloped." She shrugged and her smile brightened. "Well, congratulations anyway. You know, I think there are a couple of seats free in first class. Let me go check."

Annie tried to get the woman's attention but she'd already turned toward the front of the plane and was sashaying down the aisle. "But, ma'am—"

Grant grabbed Annie's arm. "Shh. Let her think what she wants if it means we can ride in style."

Annie shrugged. "What's the harm, right?"

"Right."

A few minutes later, they'd moved to first class and settled into the wider, leather reclining chairs. Heaven, Grant thought, happily sipping a glass of champagne the flight attendant had poured for him.

"So," Annie said, sitting a few comfortable inches away from him. He decided this would be much better than coach. After all, they weren't crammed into adjoining seats anymore. He could relax. "What jilted bride did you save?"

He leaned back into the embrace of the leather and sighed, trying to remember. "One was named Bridget. And the other was..." He shook his head. "I can't remember her name. Must have blocked it out when she broke my nose."

Annie's eyes widened, and he tried not to notice how they tilted up at the corners, giving her a mysterious, exotic look. "She broke your nose?"

He pointed at the tiny scar across the bridge of his nose where his brother's ex-fiancée's diamond ring had clipped him. "Well, she would have preferred to have broken the groom's but I was more convenient."

Annie touched the tiny, silvery scar. Her simple touch sent a shock wave through him. He needed another drink. What was wrong with him? This was his brother's fiancée—ex-fiancée!

"How did the other jilted bride react?"

His forehead folded into suspicion. "Why?"

"I just want to see if I reacted according to Miss Manners's etiquette or not."

"Pretending to get married so you can leave town with your friends thinking you're happily married is probably not the most proper reaction."

"Oh. Well, maybe I should have swooned then."

He laughed and tried to imagine this spunky bride fainting.

"So," she persisted, "tell me."

"The other bride cried."

"Is that all?" Annie sniffed.

At least she'd been more creative, Grant thought. Hell, she'd been assertive. She'd taken action. She was his kind of woman.

No, no, no. He didn't mean that.

"I wouldn't say it that way, like it was nothing. Have you ever tried to console an inconsolable, highly emotional bride? Practically shrank my suit with all that saltwater."

Annie laughed. It was a contagious sound. Frankly, he thought she'd reacted better than most under the circumstances. She hadn't gotten blubbery. She hadn't hit him, either, which was a definite plus. But she had kissed him. And he couldn't erase that from his mind. Most importantly, she'd somehow maintained her sense of humor through all of this. He'd never met anyone else like her. She intrigued and unnerved him at the same time.

"So, you know two other women who got dumped on their wedding day," she mused, sipping her champagne. "That's amazing. I mean, at least now I know I'm not the only one."

"You're definitely not the only one. Actually, they weren't about to walk down the aisle. But they were close to that when...it happened. But believe me, it was just as devastating for them. You ought to be proud. You came the closest to marrying my brother. So he must have felt—"

"They were also engaged to Griff?" Her tone skyrocketed with an explosion of disbelief.

"Sure. You mean..." Damn. He should have kept his mouth shut. "You didn't know?"

"No." Her lips compressed into a thin line.

What had he done? He'd thought she'd known. He'd thought Griffin would have at least shared his history. But then, he knew his brother. He shouldn't have assumed. And damn if he knew what to do now.

Tension coiled inside him. "Uh...look, Annie—"

She held up a hand. He noticed the slight tremor. "It's okay. I'm okay."

"Damn Griffin."

"Don't blame him. I'm as much at fault as he is." She twirled the engagement ring and the matching wedding band that Grant had placed on her finger earlier around and around.

"I doubt that."

"I simply didn't know my fiancé as well as I should have. I should have given it more time. If I ever get engaged again, I can guarantee it won't be a spur-of-the-moment decision. And I will have known the man for years and years."

"Don't be so hard on yourself."

"Well, I'd be harder on Griff if he were here. I wonder where he is. Do you know?"

"Not a clue."

"You think he's off enjoying what should have been *our* honeymoon?"

"Probably," he said, realizing she could handle the truth.

"Where were we supposed to go? Griff said he wanted to surprise me. Some surprise, huh?"

Uncomfortable with the direction of the conversation, Grant cleared his throat. "Probably Venice. It's his favorite city. It worked out so well for him the first time." He clamped his mouth closed and cursed at himself.

"You mean he went on the honeymoon without his bride before?" She stared at him, her jaw agape. "Even though he backed out of the wedding?"

"That's Griffin. That's where he met...what's her name, his second fiancée."

"Oh!" Annie plopped back in her seat and crossed her arms over her chest. "Isn't that a fine how-do-you-do? So now he's probably enjoying his third honeymoon, looking for a replacement bride again."

Damn. Why hadn't he kept a tight lid on that information? But he'd wanted her to know she hadn't lost out on much in not marrying Griffin. Still...

"So what was she like?" Annie asked.

"Who?"

"The first...the second... Both."

"Doesn't matter."

"It does to me."

Grant drew a deep breath then exhaled. *Don't do it.* But he couldn't lie and say he'd never met them.

"Come on, Grant. Tell me the truth. I can take it."

He knew she could. At least this was easier to say, and definitely truthful. "They were both blond, like you. Taller than you, but not as pretty."

Or as spunky. Or as intriguing. Of course, he didn't know how the other brides kissed—since he didn't go around kissing jilted brides every day—but he knew Annie's kiss. Oh, how he knew her kiss!

"You're just saying that to be nice." Reaching for her glass of champagne, she lifted her chin.

He met her gaze. "No, Annie, I'm not."

Something popped and sizzled between them. Then Annie looked away.

"Uh...um...when did he...Griff dump them?" she asked, her voice shaky. But he sensed it had nothing to do with Griffin this time. And that made Grant nervous.

"A few days before the wedding. One he dumped during a couples shower. That should tell you how tempted he was to marry you. I had really started to think he was going through with it this time."

"This time," she repeated, her voice soft and introspective.

He wanted to wrap his arms around her, pull her close and make her forget all about Griffin. But he didn't dare.

She shifted in her seat to look at him more fully. "Can I ask you a question?"

Another? "Sure." It's the least he could do.

"Why are you and Griff so against marriage?"

Her question stabbed at him like a blunt instrument. Instinctively, he wanted to sidestep the jab, dodge and duck to avoid it, but for some reason, probably because of Griffin, he felt like he owed her an explanation.

"Well, I wouldn't exactly put Griffin and I in the same category." He felt his shoulders tense at being compared to his twin.

He would never miss a scheduled meeting, stand up a date or walk out on his bride. If he loved someone and ever got to the unimaginable place of asking her to marry him, there would be no going back, no regrets. It would be a lifelong commitment. But he doubted he'd ever get to that point in his life. He wasn't looking for love or marriage...or anyone like Annie Baxter.

"I guess Griffin has his own reasons," he said. "I'm sure he had every intention of marrying you and...the others. But he's got extra-cold feet."

"Why?"

"I don't know." But he suspected the reasons were far too close to his own. No, no, no. He was not like Griffin. He liked being single, enjoyed his freedom. It was a simple choice. He had enough responsibilities and pressures in his job. "Maybe," he said, "Griffin figured his traveling life would be hard on a wife."

"Or fidelity would be hard on him?" Annie voiced the obvious.

"Yeah, well..." But it didn't ring any more true for Griffin than it did for Grant. There was nothing wrong with wanting to stay single. Grant had always told women straight out that he wasn't interested in anything permanent. So far, he'd managed to dodge the matrimonial bullet.

He felt Annie watching him. It was a mistake to look into her warm blue eyes filled with doubts. Damn. She was dangerous. She made him feel too much. She confused him, made him have too many hot-and-bothered ideas about her. It wasn't right. It was time to kiss...er, *say* goodbye.

Definitely no more kissing.

# 5

"WHY ARE YOU so hell-bent on breaking out of your hometown?" Grant asked, tipping his first-class chair back and stretching out his legs before him.

Trying not to notice his long, well-muscled shape, Annie stared out the plane window at the darkness that seemed to fill her soul. She felt loose, disjointed. Maybe the cause was too much champagne. Maybe it was the altitude. What were they flying at? Thirty-something thousand feet? Or maybe it was simply the stress of her wedding day settling into her.

"I've run through all the eligible bachelors in Lockett," she joked, not wanting to get into her reasons for leaving her hometown, not wanting to talk about anything seriously.

Grant's steady gaze told her he expected more.

She sighed. "Who'd marry me now?" For some reason it was easy to talk to Grant, easier even than to Aunt Maudie. "I'm a matrimonial nightmare waiting to happen. A triple-jinxed bride."

"After all that, you still want to be married?"

"Yes. No. I don't know anymore." She folded the linen napkin the flight attendant had left after picking up their dinner plates.

She'd never ridden in first class before, never knew they served things like shrimp linguini, veal Parmesan and lamb chops with mint sauce. White china plates, sparkling silverware and crystal wineglasses had made her feel special. And she'd desperately needed that this evening. Or maybe Grant and his easy banter had made her feel extraordinary.

No, it was the succulent lamb, the freshly sautéed squash, zucchini and baby carrots cut julienne style. Yes, that was it. The fresh-out-of-the-oven chocolate-chip cookies and cold milk hadn't hurt, either.

"I used to want to get married more than anything," she explained.

He was watching her, not judging, only observing in a curious way. "For marriage itself? Or was there someone special?"

"I wanted to have what my folks had—a loving relationship, a happy home, kids."

When he arched his eyebrow, she laughed.

"And Griffin knew you wanted..." His voice trailed off as if he was tripping over the idea of his brother with children.

"Kids? Yes, of course he knew. Why does that seem so strange?"

He shrugged his broad shoulder. Earlier he'd removed his tux coat. Through the starched shirt she could see the lines, planes and swells of his muscles. His shoulders looked strong, as if he would be able to comfort her if she laid her head there. But she wouldn't...couldn't. She didn't need him. She didn't need any man.

"Griffin's not the type."

"Because you're not?" she countered.

He stiffened, his shoulders squaring, his mouth thinning. "Because he's irresponsible."

"Yes, well...I know that now."

A twinkling of lights out the window caught her attention, and she leaned forward. "Look!"

"Have you ever been to New York?" Grant asked.

"No. But I've always wanted to." She wondered how many lights it took to create this dazzling array. Never had she seen anything as vast and breathtaking as this city of lights and shadows. It looked spectacular, intense, and made her heart race. "Of course, I've always wanted to go anywhere."

"What are you going to do now, Annie?" he asked, his voice softening.

She didn't want to figure everything out right now. She wanted to live moment by moment. Because if she had to look too far in the future, then she might have to examine the past—including this day—and she wasn't ready for that.

"I don't know." She added, "I guess when we land I'll find a hotel."

"I meant, are you going to return home? Move somewhere else?"

"Maybe."

"Which one?"

"Maybe I'll stay here. Maybe I won't." She drew a deep breath of the stale airline air. "I've been wanting a change. I already resigned my teaching position in Lockett, but I was waiting until after Griff and I moved to Dallas to look for a job. So I guess you could say I'm footloose and fancy free. I can do anything."

But she felt just the opposite. Something snagged her heartbeat. Good grief, she couldn't even get a groom to show up on their wedding day.

"Don't you think they'd give you your job back?" he asked.

"If I wanted it." And she realized in that moment that she didn't want to return home. "I don't. I can't really explain it. I just want to experience new things, discover life, have an adventure or two." She shrugged, unsure of her plans, her future. "So maybe I'll stay here in New York. Or maybe I'll move on." She rubbed her forehead, feeling the tightness of a headache take hold. "Do I have to decide tonight?"

"No," he said, his voice so warm and deep she thought she could have fallen in and been swallowed whole. "I didn't mean to press you."

"That's okay. You're a planner. I can tell. I bet you plan what day of the week to wash your socks."

"Actually, when to pick them up from the cleaners."

Chuckling, marveling at how different their lives were, she rested her forehead against the cool glass of the window. Her smile dimmed. Her future seemed dark, with only glimpses of possibilities ahead. "There's a whole world out there I've never explored. I want to experience it all."

But not tonight. Right now, she wanted to sleep...to forget.

"I don't think you want to experience *everything* New York has to offer."

She grinned and met his smiling eyes. Something inside her tightened then turned a notch. He had a way about him, a way of looking at her, seeing inside her, as if he knew her better than she knew herself. He somehow made her smile when she'd started to think she had nothing to smile about.

"You're probably right. I just know I'm not ready to return home yet, if ever." Tilting her head, she allowed herself to voice her fear, "Do you think a small-town girl can make it in the Big Apple?"

"It's been done before. And if anybody can, you can."

"Think so?"

"Definitely. You'll adjust. It'll just take time. That is, if you want to stay here."

She nodded, thinking, imagining, wondering what it would be like to live in New York, to call herself a New Yorker, to be one in a million, to not make the local paper's gossip column every week. Questions and doubts swirled in her head. Part of her thought it sounded like heaven. Another part of her thought it sounded awfully lonely.

"Adjust to what?" she asked.

"To the noise. Car horns blaring all night. Sirens. And the crowds. No wide-open spaces here. And then there's the native wildlife."

She arched an eyebrow in question.

"Trust me, you don't want to know. But it's nothing like the deer and antelope you have back in Texas."

"We don't have antelope, at least not in Lockett. Maybe an armadillo, or a better bet is a rattlesnake."

He laughed.

"What else?" she asked.

"It can get damn cold in the winter, and hot in summer. The sun reflects off all the buildings and concrete."

"You can't scare me away from hot weather. I'm a Texan."

"I'm not trying to scare you." He touched her arm and a warm shiver rippled through her. "But it's a different heat up here."

It was different all right, she thought as her temperature went up ten degrees because of his touch.

"Especially," he said, "when you consider air-conditioning."

"Air-conditioning?"

"Some places don't have it. Better ask before you sign a lease."

"I'll keep that in mind."

She realized Grant made her nervous, excited, vibrant. She felt an uneasiness fill her. She'd just been dumped by his brother. She shouldn't be attracted to him—to anyone, but especially him. After all, she knew up front he was antimatrimony.

"You have to realize," he said, "you're not in Kansas anymore, Dorothy."

"Yeah—" she grinned "—isn't it wonderful!"

IT WAS THE LEAST he could do, Grant rationalized as he heaved Annie's heavy luggage into the trunk of the waiting cab. The cacophony of New York sounds surrounded him. Exhaust fumes choked him. A horn blasted. A man with a Brooklyn accent cursed when a taxi ignored him. But there was an energy that seemed to vibrate through the air, making Grant pick up his pace.

Texas had slowed him down temporarily...or, at least, his thoughts, his reactions. Maybe that's how Annie had talked him into being her temporary groom. Now he was home and it was time to get back to work, to get away from Annie. His mind started to click with all the things he needed to do at the office come Monday. But until then, he had to get Annie settled. In a hotel. Alone.

In the space of a few minutes, the taxi chugged through traffic, heading into The City. He sat beside Annie, who leaned forward, looking toward the driver.

"So, have you lived in New York long?" she asked the driver. Suddenly her accent sounded shameless, conspicuous. And it could get her in trouble.

The cabdriver turned and looked at her as if she was a nut. Nobody talked to cabdrivers. But clearly, Annie's smile disarmed him. Grant made a mental note to tell her she had to be careful who she spoke with, who she smiled at.

"I live here three years," he said, his Latino accent heavy and thick but friendly with a sunny warmth.

"And do you like it?" she asked.

"Like it? I suppose. Sure. Why not?"

"Well, you could live somewhere else."

"Make money here," the driver said.

"I see. And do you have a family?" she asked.

He nodded, slammed on his brakes, blasted his horn and swerved into the next lane all in one motion. The action jolted Annie back into her seat, practically onto Grant's lap. Her hand grabbed his thigh. His nerves shattered in confusion.

What was he doing here with Annie, wanting her? He should have left her in Texas where she belonged. Bringing her was only going to cause trouble.

As quickly as she'd given his libido a shake, she shifted gears, ignoring him, and gazed out the passenger window, staring up at the darkened skyscrapers. He could imagine her mouth gaping open; her eyes widening with wonder. She had an innocent charm, a disarming beauty that he should forget, ignore. But he couldn't. He couldn't stop watching her. He couldn't stop wanting to kiss her again.

"Would you look at that!" she exclaimed. "Is that what I think it is?"

Grateful for the distraction, Grant bent forward and followed her gaze up along the steel structure. "The Empire State Building?"

"Oh, how romantic!"

He'd never heard it described that way. But then he'd never been sight-seeing with anyone like Annie. She was a foreigner in this jungle of streets and buildings; she'd get gobbled up quick if she were left alone.

Damn. With that thought, he knew what he'd have to do—not that he wanted to do it, but he had no choice. It was all Griffin's fault.

Tapping on the front seat, he snagged the driver's attention and gave him his apartment address. The driver made a U-turn in the middle of Thirty-fourth Street. Annie gasped and reached for Grant.

He did the only thing he could. He folded her hand in his. She entwined her fingers with his, clasping his hand, pulling it toward her.

"Is this safe?" she asked. "I mean—"

"We're okay," he reassured her. But he knew they weren't okay. He wasn't okay. This was definitely dangerous territory. The touch of her soft, supple skin against his made him think of everything but reassuring her. He had a completely different reason for holding her hand now, a selfish one.

What the hell was he going to do with her?

If he was smart, he'd send her—along with her luggage, wedding dress and dreams—straight back to Texas where she belonged. Away from him.

"THIS IS YOUR PLACE?" Annie asked, standing outside his apartment door in her wedding attire. She already held half a hot dog in her hand that she'd purchased from a nearby street vendor. "I can't stay here."

"Why not?" He nudged the door open with his shoulder. "Where else are you going to stay?"

"I don't know." She sounded nervous, her voice strained. "But I'll figure something out. There's bound to be a hotel nearby."

"Dozens. But why waste your money? This place is free."

"Not for you."

"Come on. I won't bite." Although he wouldn't mind taking a nibble...along her neck...behind her knee...

"But—"

He left her standing in the hallway and entered his apartment. Striding through the living room, he deposited her bags in the bedroom. When he returned to the foyer, she'd eased inside, barely. He moved her train and veil out of the way and shut the door, trying not to think about being alone—totally alone—with this woman who had a strange effect on him.

Watching her swallow the last of her hot dog, he asked, "Want something to wash that artery-clogger down with?"

The tension seemed to drain from her face, and the corners of her eyes crinkled with the hint of a smile. "Sure. Do you have any soda?"

"Doubtful. No milk, either. I'll go get—"

"No, that's okay. Water is fine. I don't want to be a bother."

"You're not." But she was. Or his thoughts about

her were bothersome, worrisome, nerve-racking. "Come on in. Kick your shoes off. This isn't Texas but we Yankees can be just as friendly."

She arched an eyebrow at him.

"I meant...hell, we've got manners, too. Look, Annie, I don't want you to worry about staying here. I'm not after anything. I won't bother you."

"Thanks a lot. Another blow to my ego today."

He shoved his fingers through his hair. He wasn't handling this right. "I want to help you. Set things right. After all, my brother is the one who—"

"Look out," she said, her voice tight with bitter humor, "here comes the sympathy vote." Propping her hands on her hips, she glared at him. "I told you I don't need your help, or your sympathy, or your guilt. I'll be fine. I'm great at rebounding."

Her words seemed to freeze in the air. Had she just admitted she hadn't loved Griffin? Why didn't that make him feel relieved?

"Annie, don't get all flustered. You're tired. I'm tired. And before we say something we'll regret, why don't you go take a hot bath and relax? Tomorrow we can sort all of this out. If you still want to go to a hotel then I'll find you one."

He moved toward her cautiously, as if he wasn't quite sure how she would react to being crowded. Slowly, he placed his hands on her narrow shoulders and turned her toward his bedroom. "Through that door you'll find the bath. Make yourself at home. I'll rummage us up some dinner." Then he thought about the hot dog she'd eaten. "Or are you full?"

"Oh, no. I could eat."

He grinned. Somehow he knew she was going to get through this ordeal just fine. But was he?

A few minutes later, he heard the water running as she filled the tub. He busied himself in the kitchen. He opened the refrigerator but the shelves were basically bare—just as Annie was probably naked in the bathtub by now.

His throat went dry and he remembered seeing her for the first time. She might as well have been wearing nothing at all what with that skimpy lingerie that showed more bare skin than it covered.

"Grant?"

Startled, he turned and found Annie standing in the doorway, still in her wedding dress.

"There are towels—"

She held up a little metal object. "I need your help."

"With?"

She presented him with her back. "I can't undo the buttons."

He noticed the long row of satin-covered buttons trailing down her spine. The first one had been unfastened. The second was missing. He could do this. He'd just shut off his mind, pretend it was a stock report he was reading. *Yeah, right.*

"What's this?" he asked, taking the metal thing from her.

"My aunt uses it to crochet. Use it to unfasten the buttons. Believe me, it's the only way."

It took him several minutes to get the hang of it. His focus narrowed. Perspiration popped out along his forehead. He could do this—any seven-year-old could! Dammit. Finally, the buttons loosened and he made his way down her back. He almost forgot what he was doing until he saw her bra strap. He swallowed hard and continued along the sloping curve of her spine where her waist narrowed. *A few more buttons, that's all. You can do it. Just concentrate. Forget you're undressing a beautiful, desirable woman. A woman you've already kissed.*

He mopped his brow with his shirt sleeve, then proceeded. He refused to look at her silky skin, to breathe in her warm exotic scent. Wrestling with the third to last button, he leaned closer, frowned, then realized his hand was resting on her bottom, her well-shaped bottom. He stopped, stared and tried to swallow.

"Grant? Is there a problem?"

Definitely.

"All done," he said, thrusting the crochet hook at her. He backed away before he couldn't.

"Thanks." Without turning around she left the kitchen.

Jerking his attention back to the refrigerator, he stared at the only contents—a carton of expired milk, a couple of bottles of beer, one egg and a few withering grapes. The cool air helped chill his overactive imagination.

He imagined her slipping the wedding gown off her shoulders, the satin pooling at her feet. He knew all too well what she was wearing underneath all that virginal white. It certainly wasn't virginal.

Giving himself a mental shake, he tried to think what Annie would want—not what he wanted, which was Annie—and he reached for the phone and ordered a pizza.

Before it arrived, Annie stepped out of the bedroom. She wore a pale pink satin robe that was cinched at the waist. It flowed over her limbs, emphasized and exaggerated her curves. Her skin looked warm, moist, flushed from the hot bath. His throat contracted. His abdomen tightened with need. He almost groaned aloud. What the hell was she doing to him?

Her hand closed the gap at the top of the robe, erasing the tiny glimpse of lace underneath. "I'm sorry. I didn't have anything else..." She glanced down at her feet, curled her toes into his carpet. "I was supposed to be on my honeymoon."

*Don't remind me.*

She moved past him and he caught a whiff of gardenia. She must have found the bubble bath one of his ex-girlfriends had left.

A knock on the door made her freeze.

"Who's that?" she asked, her voice strained. "Could it be...Griff?" she whispered, panic tightening the corners of her mouth.

"Nah. What would he be doing here? It's probably the pizza deliveryman."

"Pizza?" Her eyes brightened. "Delivered here? Right to your door?"

"Yeah."

She blushed. "We don't have that service in Lockett. I've always wanted to order pizza to be delivered."

"It's the eighth wonder of the world." He grinned and opened the door. His smile disappeared. "Mrs. Hennessey!"

"Oh, Grant! Congratulations, my dear." The older woman plowed right inside his apartment and shoved a dusty bottle of champagne into his hands. "I saw you and your bride arrive this evening. And I just couldn't believe my eyes. Grant Stevens married! I didn't even know you were engaged. I thought you were still seeing Sus—"

"Mrs. Hennessey," he said abruptly, "this is Annie." He indicated the woman standing near him. The nearly naked woman standing in his apartment. His heart pounded. She should have been his sister-in-law, but she looked more like a Victoria's Secret model. She looked anything but sweet and naive.

"Uh—" he cleared his throat "—Annie, this is my landlady."

"Oh. Hello." Her blush deepened.

"Why, I'm so sorry to intrude. I can see you two have...are...well, are busy." The elderly woman coughed and started backing toward the door.

"Mrs. Hennessey," Annie said, stepping forward.

Grant caught a glimpse of her long, lean leg that had him imagining things he definitely shouldn't be thinking about his sister-in-law. *But she's not your sister-in-law. She's not even dating your brother anymore. She's free and clear.*

"I'm afraid," Annie continued, oblivious to his discomfort, "there's been a misunderstanding—"

"Annie, darling," Grant said, wrapping his arm around her waist. It was a rash decision. He would have been better off thinking it through rather than acting impulsively. But at the moment, it all made sense. He pulled her against his side. "Mrs. Hennessey doesn't want to hear about our little disagreement. I told you I'd take some time off work soon and give you the honeymoon you deserve. But until then..."

He dipped his head and touched his lips to hers, briefly, but long enough to stir a need inside him. Her lips were so soft. Her body was so warm. He was so confused.

"It was a whirlwind romance," he said, his voice deeper and huskier than he'd intended. Glancing down at his make-believe bride, he struggled to think straight. "Wasn't it, darling?"

"Oh, yes," she breathed, as if equally affected by him. Could she be? Or was she thinking of him as Griffin?

Damn. That thought shocked him like a bucket of ice water. Anger flooded him. He wasn't his brother. And for a crazy second, he wanted to prove to her the difference.

He kissed her again, this time deeper, slower, more fully. Her mouth felt stiff at first, resistant, then she opened to him. Her body relaxed against him. Her arms slipped around his neck to pull him closer.

Barely over the pounding of his heart, he heard Mrs. Hennessey whisper, "Oh, my! I'll just leave you two alone now. Congratulations again."

Then the door clicked shut. And he kept right on kissing Annie. This time, without an audience.

# 6

*OH MY HEAVENS!* Annie felt herself sinking into Grant, falling deeper, deeper... His mouth made her limbs go weak with yearnings she couldn't assimilate or comprehend. Had she ever felt like this?

With Rodney, her first fiancé? No way. He hadn't been very accomplished at kissing. But he'd been sweet, tender.

What about Travis, her second? Nope. He'd been a good kisser, but even his knock-your-socks-off technique hadn't taken her breath away.

And Griffin? Well, he didn't come close.

Grant deepened the kiss, his tongue teasing hers, his mouth hot, gentle, yet demanding. She clung to him for support, kissed him like there was no tomorrow, like there hadn't been a today. A today when she was supposed to have married his brother! A splash of reality gave her a chill.

"Oh. Oh, dear. Oh, my!" She pushed away from Grant.

Wild emotions tangled her thoughts. She felt her cheeks burn with embarrassment and confusion. What kind of woman was she? Could she fall in and out of love that quickly? What would Grant think of her?

Her spine straightened. Why on earth should it matter what he thought anyway?

She needed air. She needed space. She needed to get a hold of herself.

It would have been so easy to succumb to the sexual desires that Grant stirred. What was wrong with her? Had she lost her mind? Was she that desperate that she couldn't wait for Griffin's memory to grow cold before she sought a replacement? Maybe it was simply that this was her wedding night—or supposed to be. And Griffin had simply primed the pump, so to speak.

Or maybe it was Grant. No, she couldn't—wouldn't—accept that theory.

"Wh-where's Mrs....your landlady?"

"She left. Didn't you hear her say goodbye?"

She hadn't heard anything but the beating of her own heart.

"Look, Annie, I'm sorry about all that." He took a step away from her.

Her mind felt sluggish, and she blinked, trying to grasp his meaning, his reasons for a quick apology. Guilt? Regret? She should feel both, but she didn't. "You're sorry for kissing me?"

He jammed his hands in his trouser pockets. "For saying we're married."

"Oh, yeah." *That!* It was the least of her worries. What concerned her more was why she'd so readily jumped back into the part of his bride. "Well, you didn't exactly. Your landlady inferred it. But I guess now we're even."

"Maybe." The low rumble in his chest made her pulse quicken.

"So, uh," she stuttered, like her emotions, "you want to share why we're back to our charade? This time for your benefit. I can't believe it's illegal in New

York for two single adults to be staying under the same roof."

He chuckled but crossed his arms over his chest. He seemed restless, antsy, awkward, as if he wasn't sure how to act in his own apartment. She remembered the feel of his chest against hers, the strength there, the way she'd wanted to run her hands over his firm muscles, his taut skin...his bare skin. Giving herself a mental shake, she tried to think of something else.

*Yeah, right.*

She made an aboutface and studied the books lining the shelves along one wall of Grant's apartment. Wall Street. Business. Sam Walton. Harvard. Words jumped out at her but she couldn't focus on anything but the man behind her.

"Mrs. Hennessey," he said, "is the resident matchmaker, and a horrible one at that. She's got more granddaughters and great-nieces than Mother Hubbard."

Annie slanted her gaze at a prime specimen most mothers would be thrilled to have interested in their daughter. "I assume she's set you up a few times."

"Once or twice. She's not very subtle. She'll get one of her nieces dolled up and bring her right to my door. They'll stand their together waiting, expectant, like I've got a glass slipper or engagement ring in my pocket."

She laughed but she felt a strange, fleeting emotion tug at her when she imagined Grant out with another woman...kissing someone else...making love to... *Stop! You're being ridiculous.* "And have you been out with any of her nieces?"

"I'm not that desperate."

Was she? No. That's not why she'd kissed Grant. But she wasn't clear on the reason and didn't want to search any further. It was better to forget the kisses, forget Grant.

"Mrs. Hennessey," she said, "mentioned something about how she thought you were still seeing someone." She heard the question, felt the stitch of jealousy.

Grant rubbed the back of his neck. "Oh, that was nothing. All over now."

*Good. Very good.* Not that it mattered if Grant was seeing anyone or not. She wasn't interested. And she'd keep her hands to herself from now on.

"I might have even played the relationship up a bit in front of Mrs. Hennessey, for her benefit."

"Or for your own," Annie countered.

"Exactly. That's why when she showed up here tonight, having seen us dressed in our wedding attire, I figured I'd let her go right on thinking we were married. Maybe it'll give me a reprieve for a while. Later, after you've gotten settled somewhere, she'll think I'm divorced and, I hope, undesirable."

"I doubt it." How could anyone think of Grant that way? She was certainly having trouble imagining it at the moment.

He jingled the change in his pocket. "I should have asked your permission before I dragged you into this. You at least gave me that courtesy."

"And here I thought I'd hog-tied you."

"I never do anything I don't want to do."

*Really!* A self-satisfied smile tugged at her mouth. Feeling bold and foolish, she couldn't resist saying, "Tell me this then—why'd you kiss me? Just for effect?"

Or was it something more? Or was she trying to make the kiss out to be more than it was? What was wrong with her? She should be banning men from her life, not be willing to jump into another man's arms the minute she got left at the altar.

But Grant was like Sir Lancelot, riding in, carrying her to safety. He'd saved her butt in Lockett. He'd helped her in more ways than she could ever thank him. Maybe her gratitude was the reason for her attraction to him.

Or possibly it was his breathtaking kisses.

"I'm sorry about that...kiss." He rubbed the back of his neck.

"Sorry?" Her temples pounded.

*Oh, great!* Not exactly the answer she'd been hoping for. What had she wanted? A declaration of love? No way! "I've never had a man apologize for kissing me." She leaned her head into her hands. "Could my life get any worse?"

"Annie—"

"Please." She turned and walked toward a far window. "Don't apologize again."

She stared down at the headlights traveling along the street below. The tops of the cars looked like tiny bugs scuttling about as they switched lanes and sped through lights. She wished she could zip into a new lane...or new life...as easily. She wished she was anywhere but here at the moment. A chill rippled through her.

Why did Grant's kiss matter so much? And why did his motive—or lack thereof—matter? What was wrong with her?

"Are you okay?" he asked. He moved to stand close

to her. Too close. If she turned, she'd brush against him. If he wanted, all he had to do was reach out to touch her. It shocked her to realize she wanted him to touch her, hold her, kiss her. But for comfort, or something else?

*Definitely something else.*

A trembling started deep inside her. "Yeah, I'm okay." But she wasn't. "This has just been one hell of a day."

Her voice snagged on raw emotions. Her nerves felt jagged and sharp, like a serrated knife's edge. Oh, how far she'd come in one day.

This morning she'd woken with the prospect of walking down the aisle, getting married and flying off on her honeymoon. As the day had progressed, her life had become more complicated and more wretched. Now, here she was in New York City. She'd never felt so lost, so alone, so dejected. Not only had Griff rejected her, but now so had his brother!

Disbelief turned to despair. She felt her heart caving in on itself. A smothering sensation made her throat constrict. All the tension and stress from the day piled on top of her. Tears scalded the backs of her eyes. She squeezed them shut, tried to shut down her emotions. But hot tears seeped through her lashes, burning a path down her cheeks.

"Here I am," she said, her voice as broken as her spirit, "standing in a stranger's apartment..." she gulped air and gestured wildly "...and I'm supposed to be on...on...m-m-my honeymoon!" Her shoulders shook with suppressed tears.

"Annie—" Grant's voice sounded deep and warm

"—would you really want to be married to Griffin right now?"

*That wasn't the point!*

Tears came harder, faster. She pressed her fists to her eyes. She didn't want to cry. She wouldn't, dammit. But no amount of pressure could stop the flow. Once they started, they were like a free-flowing, spring-fed fountain, with a deep reservoir of pain to draw from.

The next thing she knew she was sitting on the floor, her satin robe, that she'd traveled to Amarillo to buy, ballooned around her legs. She felt Grant's strong hands grip her shoulders.

Nothing she ever planned came true. None of her dreams. None of her fantasies. Why did men run from her?

When her sobs turned to gurgly hiccups, her chest aching from the release, she met Grant's concerned gaze. The corners of his eyes were pinched, tiny lines angling out toward his hairline.

"Have you ever met a more pathetic woman?" she asked, trying to lighten the mood.

"Yeah."

His answer intrigued her. "Who?"

"Griffin's first fiancée. She crumbled like a wadded-up tissue, a soggy one. Her life revolved around Griffin's. Yours doesn't. Didn't. That's why I know you're going to be fine without him. Better, in fact."

"Yeah?" Her voice warbled. "You know what it feels like to be number three?"

"Better than number four?"

Her mouth cracked with a half smile. "You think there will be a number four?"

"No doubt about it." He wrapped his arm around her shoulder and pulled her close against his chest. They sat on the floor together, their limbs pretzeling as he tried to offer comfort, and she drew from his strength, his humor, his optimism. "Griffin's the pathetic one. He can't commit. He wants to, but he just can't. And you...well, he came closer to marrying you than anyone else."

"Yeah, but..."

"What?" he asked when she couldn't finish the question. He peered down at her, his warm breath fanning her face, his mouth so close she could have easily touched her lips to his. But she didn't.

"Nothing." She should move away. "Never mind."

"No, go ahead. What were you going to say?"

She dipped her chin, embarrassed to ask the question spinning around her brain. Yet at the same time she wanted—needed—to know the answer. "What's wrong with me?"

The tone in her voice slashed through Grant's own defenses. Vulnerability shone in her tear-stained eyes. With his thumb, he wiped away a stray tear and smear of mascara. His finger trailed down the slope of her cheek, the curve of her jaw, until his gaze landed on her trembling mouth. Tears glistened, making the rosy hue of her lips look like dewy petals. His gut twisted with need. But he fought the desire, tried to focus on her needs, not his own.

"Nothing's wrong with you, Annie. Believe me."

"I wish I could. Three men have dumped me at the altar. There has to be something wrong with me! I jumped into these relationships. No one coerced me, as I coerced you today. Who else is there to blame but me?"

"Maybe no one. Maybe none of them was the right one for you."

She stared at him, a swirl of dark emotions welling in eyes that looked soft, defenseless, glowing. The vivid blue deepened to midnight, dark and mysterious. "But there has to be something. Why else...?"

He pressed his finger to her lips to silence her questions. What was the point of torturing herself this way? "Believe me, Annie, there's nothing wrong with you. Any man would want you, desire you."

She swallowed hard. "Even you?"

His chest felt tight, but not as rigid as another part of his anatomy. He nodded.

"I don't believe you." Her voice cracked. "You were the one who apologized for kissing me."

It was an accusatory statement, but it revealed her vulnerability, her insecurity. He felt like a jerk for causing her more pain. And he knew of only one solution.

"I'm not apologizing now." He dipped his head and captured her mouth. She was soft, pliant and, oh, so warm. He folded her within his arms and delved deeply, sinking into her, drawing from her, sampling the different textures of her mouth.

She offered. He took.

He gave. She demanded more.

What began as a gentle kiss turned greedy, obsessive. He couldn't control himself. His hands roamed over her, luxuriating in the satin material that was the only barrier between them. Sometimes he couldn't tell where the satin ended and she began. Her skin was smooth and soft and hot to his touch. He bracketed her shoulders, slid his palms down her arms, then his fingers drew a random line up the inside of her wrist and came to rest at the narrow indentation of her waist.

She leaned into him, arched her breasts against him. He could feel the pebbled points through her robe and his shirt. Slowly, a delicious need building inside him, he moved his hand up along her rib cage to cup her breast. The weight settled against his palm and he gently flicked his thumb against the nipple. A low moan escaped her.

A knock on the door separated them like oil and water.

Annie folded her arms over her chest, clutched the robe tighter against her throat. Her eyes were wide with uncertainty, shock and...annoyance? He wondered if she would have stopped him before...

"Could that be Mrs. Hennessey again?" she asked in a hoarse whisper.

"Probably the pizza I ordered."

"Oh, yeah." She pushed to her feet, her hand clutching the window ledge. "You must be hungry."

He stood, too. His gaze locked with hers. "Yeah."

But it sure wasn't for pepperoni or extra cheese. Whatever it was, it was definitely forbidden.

She curled her bare toes into the carpet and looked away. "Shouldn't you answer the door?"

He'd rather ignore the intruder but he knew he wouldn't be able to pick up where he and Annie had left off. Not now. It was better this way; he should stay away from her. She was vulnerable. He was crazy.

Walking stiffly, he moved to open the door. "What the hell?"

"Hello, big brother," Griffin said, standing in the doorway, suitcase in hand. "Can you put me up for the night?"

# 7

"WHAT THE HELL are you doing here?" Grant asked, his voice gruff with anger.

Annie's skin prickled. What was wrong? Who was it? An old girlfriend? Certainly not the pizza delivery man! Wrapping her skimpy robe more securely around her, for decorum's sake and to squelch her desire for Grant, she took a step sideways and peered around his broad shoulder.

"Griff!" The air rushed out of her. She felt her body go numb. She clutched the knot holding her robe closed. The robe she was supposed to have been wearing for him...on their honeymoon!

Guilt twisted her insides. She rubbed away the taste of Grant's kiss. Then she straightened her spine. What did she have to feel guilty for? He was no longer her fiancé. It was, after all, Griffin's fault. If he hadn't dumped her at the altar, she wouldn't be here in New York with his brother. And they wouldn't have been kissing. She admitted there were a few leaps of logic but she didn't care.

"What are you doing here?" she asked, now irritated that he'd intruded.

Her ex-fiancé's stunned gaze locked on her. "Annie?" He gulped. His Adam's apple plunged then surfaced, as if he was unsure if she'd wallop him—as he deserved. "What are *you* doing here?"

"Where did you want me to be? Back home in Lockett? Still waiting for you at the altar?"

"Annie—"

Grant pressed his hand against his brother's chest. "It doesn't matter what she's doing here. It's none of your business." His hand folded into a tight fist, crushing the front of Griffin's shirt. His arm cocked back as if he was about to take a punch. "But I'll tell you what I'm gonna do!"

Common sense and decency returned, and Annie grabbed Grant's arm, felt his muscles bulge beneath her fingertips. "It's okay, Grant. Really."

"No, it isn't," he said through gritted teeth.

The two men stared at each other. Twin brothers. She'd once thought they looked exactly alike. But she'd been wrong. There was a strength in Grant, an embarrassing weakness in Griffin. Why hadn't she seen it before? Because she'd never had a chance to compare and contrast them in person.

Even after meeting Grant, she hadn't wanted to see the differences even though he'd pointed out several significant distinctions between him and his brother. Now the truth was like unfiltered sunlight glaring down on her ex-fiancé. She saw every freckle, every crinkle, every glittering gray strand that had begun to lighten Griffin's dark brown hair.

Her ex-fiancé stepped back toward the elevators as though he was going to make a run for it. "I, um, shouldn't have come here. But I didn't know—"

"It's all right, Griff," she repeated, her voice calmer than she would have ever dreamed—if she'd ever dreamed this type of scenario, which she hadn't. "Come in."

"No." Grant blocked the doorway.

"Grant!" she scolded. She realized then he was defending her in a caveman sort of way. Defending her! When had anyone ever done that? Something softened inside her.

She put her hand gently on his arm, gaining his attention. "I know this is hard for all of us, but maybe it's for the best. Why don't you give Griff and I a few minutes alone? This is between us."

"Uh," Griffin said, his eyes widening, "that's not necessary. I, uh—"

"Yes, it is," Grant said. "If Annie wants to talk to you, then you're gonna listen. If she wants me to hold you while she kicks the sh—"

"Grant!" Trying to soften her tone, she added, "Griff, I think we have a few things to say to each other."

Her ex-fiancé stared at her like she might try to push him out of the seventh-story window. A bubble of laughter rose within her and she swallowed it. A few hours ago she might have considered such a form of retaliation. But the flight and her time spent with Grant had changed her perspective.

"Are you sure about this, Annie?" Grant asked.

"It'll be all right. I won't hurt your brother too badly." She grinned and sent Grant a wink.

He frowned but not as deeply as his brother. "I'm not worried about *him*." His hands bracketed her shoulders. "Are you sure *you* are up for this?"

"I'm fine." Better than she would have ever imagined. She felt a Zenlike calmness flow through her veins.

When she glanced at Griff, who had a politician-caught-with-his-hand-in-the-funds kind of look, she only felt a mild irritation toward him. It wasn't because he'd run out on her right before their wedding. She realized with horror that it was because he'd interrupted her kiss—or whatever it had been about to evolve into—with Grant, his brother!

"Okay, then," Grant said. "If you need me, Annie, I'll be in my bedroom." He turned a sour look on his brother. "Watch yourself. Understand?"

Several minutes later, fortified with a slice of fresh pizza which had just arrived, Annie faced her ex-fiancé alone. "Don't look so worried, Griff. I won't bite."

"Yeah, well...I can see you're covering up a lot of hurt with that pizza. I can't blame you for that. But you better watch how much junk food you eat."

"Are you saying you care if I pack on a few extra pounds?"

"Sure, I care!"

"Good." She took a huge bite of the cheesy, greasy pizza and knew Griff didn't have a clue how bad his words had made him sound.

"So, did you forget where you were supposed to be this morning, Griff?"

He faced her, his arms stretched out wide, and grinned, that old grin that she'd once thought charming. Now it reminded her of a little boy who was used to getting away with things. Not this time.

"Annie, I—"

"Save it, Griff. I really don't care what your reasons are...were. It doesn't matter anymore. Or maybe it never did. I just wanted to thank you."

"Excuse me?"

"You heard me correctly," she said around another bite. "Thank you. What you did this morning—er, didn't do—by not showing up for our wedding, by running away...well, you saved me from making a terrible mistake."

"What's the catch? You gonna sue me or something now?"

She laughed. "No, not at all."

She moved forward and placed the diamond-studded wedding set across his palm. Grant had told her she had every right to keep it. She could sell it for money, which would come in handy as she made a new life for herself, but it didn't feel right. She didn't want Griff or his rings.

"I'm not angry with you, Griff. Honest."

"Uh-huh." His eyes narrowed with disbelief, but he pocketed the rings.

"Fact is," she said, her voice lifting with an extra dose of optimism, "I'm delighted by the prospects."

His gaze slid toward the closed door of Grant's bedroom. "With my brother? What the hell has he been doing? Moving in while my back was turned?"

"Griff, I think you gave up all rights to any jealousy or possessiveness when you ran out of Lockett this morning. But don't worry. There's nothing between your brother and me."

Nothing but a few kisses and way too many hormones. Wishes and fantasies, she thought, which could disappear as easily as a bridegroom.

"Then, is this some kind of joke? Your thanking me?"

"Not at all. I'm glad we didn't get married."

He took a step toward her, his gaze softening, giving her a glimmer of the man she'd fallen in love with. She felt a tug deep inside her but cut the thread with a sharp recollection of his betrayal.

"Annie, darlin'," he said, his voice imploring, "I was wrong. I shouldn't have treated you that way. I should have—"

"What?" She laughed. "Married me?" She shook her head. "No, Griff. You were right. We weren't right for each other. I can see that now. We were too hasty. Time would have shown us that. See, you saved us a lot of time and heartache."

"Annie." He cupped her elbows and pulled her close. Her pizza mashed against the front of his shirt, orange grease staining the starched white cotton. Frowning, he pulled the pizza out of her hand, tossed it onto the top of the box and slid his arms around her waist. She braced her hands against his chest to keep her distance and the pepperoni stain off her satin robe. Strange, the feel of him didn't make her heart race. She noticed he wasn't as muscular as Grant when he pulled her close. She could feel Griff's breath hot and urgent on her neck. His eyes closed as he bent to kiss her.

Her eyes remained open; her heart detached. Her brain analyzed the kiss as if they were a couple on television. She felt his lips move against her, his hands at her waist urging her closer.

She wasn't repulsed; she wasn't interested, either. Her brain didn't fog. Her pulse didn't skitter. Her body didn't melt. He didn't have Grant's finesse, didn't wear the same cologne, either. Such a shame. Because Grant's scent made something inside her yearn for more. And his kiss made her knees weak.

Griffin, she decided, didn't affect her at all.

With a slight push, she moved away from her ex-fiancé. "You better be going."

He blinked. "What's wrong, baby?"

"Nothing." And she meant it. She felt somehow empowered, in control of her own life. "Goodbye, Griff."

"Goodbye? You can't stay here," he said, the bridge of his nose crinkling with disgust, "with my brother!"

"I'm tired and need a good night's sleep. Tomorrow, I'm going to look for a place to live."

"Here?"

She nodded. "That's right."

"You don't belong in New York City!"

"Maybe not. But then maybe I do. Nobody can decide that but me." She opened the door. "Now, good night, Griffin. And goodbye."

"I'LL SEE HIM OUT," Grant said, leaving his bedroom behind and walking through the living area, over the Oriental rug and past the wall of windows looking out onto Central Park. He caught Annie's shocked glance. "Yes, I was listening. So shoot me."

"You heard everything?" she asked. Something in her voice told him she wasn't speaking of the last words she'd said to his brother. The silence during their kiss came back to him. His body tensed once more.

"I heard enough." He wasn't about to admit he'd grabbed the door handle when Griffin had kissed her. A red-hot anger had blinded him. It had taken all his strength and pride to resist walking out and sucker-punching his brother. He was just trying to protect Annie. Somebody had to!

"I'll be back in a minute," he said, clapping his brother on the shoulder and escorting him to the door. "Don't open the door for anybody," he called over his shoulder.

She wore a thin smile. "Why? You expecting an ex-girlfriend or somebody to show up next?"

"I'll be right back." It would be my luck, he thought as they headed to the elevator, if Susan showed up next. "Save me some of that pizza."

"You better hurry then."

Grant stepped into the elevator with his brother. He hoped this was their last visitor for the evening, their last surprise. Damn, he should have told Annie not to answer the phone, either. He doubted Susan would show up at his apartment, but she might call. And he didn't relish the idea of explaining Annie to Susan or vice versa.

The explanation to Annie would be simple enough. Susan was an ex-girlfriend. Nothing serious. But now she was a mega-client. This account could mean everything to him. Every red-blooded American dream of success, wealth beyond even Grant's wildest imaginings would be his. And he didn't need anything, or anyone, to disrupt business—including a jealous ex-lover.

He'd never felt comfortable with a woman once he broke up with her. How did one become friends after being intimate, then not? Normally, he would have kept his distance from Susan, but she'd made him a proposition he couldn't refuse. A business proposition, that is. He secretly thought she wanted more after he took her company public. He'd deal with that later...much later. But explaining Annie might be damn tough in the meantime, especially because she confused the hell out of him.

How did he explain that?

"Goodbye, Annie," Griffin said as the doors of the elevator slid closed. In a confidential tone, he added for Grant only, "She's depressed."

"Why do you think that?"

"The pizza. Already drowning her sorrows in junk food."

Grant bit back a laugh. He remembered Annie chowing down on French fries before the wedding, before she knew her fiancé had taken a long walk in the other direction. But as usual, Griffin had every explanation wrapped around his own ego.

"I made a mistake," he said.

"I'll say." Grant nodded. "Why the hell did you come here? Why aren't you in Paris or Venice or where-the-hell-ever by now?"

He shrugged. "It didn't seem right once I arrived in New York, so I canceled my international flight."

A silence settled between them. They'd never been close. Grant had always felt more than a couple of minutes older than Griffin. And Griffin had always behaved more than a couple of minutes younger.

"But that's not the mistake I made," he said.

Grant looked at his brother, knowing full well he didn't want to know the answer to the silent question bouncing between them like a Ping-Pong ball. A sick feeling settled in his stomach. A muscle in his jaw clenched.

"I shouldn't have walked away from Annie. Hell, she's the best thing that ever happened to me," Griffin said. Grant wasn't about to say the same. But he knew it was true. Or he was beginning to recognize the impact she'd already had on his life. "I should have married her."

"Too late now." *I married her.* But Grant would keep that part secret. Besides, the marriage wasn't legal. It certainly wasn't the forever-and-ever kind. Hell, it was already over as far as he was concerned.

Until his landlady came around.

Until Annie needed him again.

"You don't think she'd forgive me?" Griffin asked.

"What woman in her right mind would?"

Griffin crossed his arms over his chest. His suitcase sat at his feet like a puppy dog. Only Griffin would have never taken the responsibility for a dog—or a wife, for that matter. So what did Grant have to worry about? Griffin could think he'd made a mistake all he wanted. It didn't change the fact that Annie was in *Grant's* apartment, in *his* bed. Or she would be tonight. Problem was, Grant wouldn't be sharing it with her.

Not yet, he thought. It surprised him how much he wanted Annie in his bed. In his life. Permanently. What was the matter with him? He didn't want marriage. He didn't want Annie.

Okay, he knew that wasn't true. He wanted her. But he couldn't have her.

"Annie's not like other women," Griffin stated.

No one had to tell Grant that.

"She didn't seem too angry tonight," Griffin added, more to himself than for Grant's benefit.

"Yeah," Grant said with a waspish chuckle. "She's relieved she's not in Venice with you on a honeymoon."

"I don't think so." Griffin rubbed his jaw. There was

a thick stubble advertising that he hadn't shaved today. Obviously he hadn't even thought of attending his own wedding earlier. He'd simply been on the run. "I think she's confused, hurt. And I bet I can win her back."

Grant shook his head, knowing what was coming next. The muscles along his neck tightened.

"With your help, that is, big brother."

"No."

Griffin looked at him, that wide-eyed innocent look that had always made Grant acquiesce—but not this time.

"Why?" Griffin asked.

Grant imagined shoving his brother up against the wall and telling him to stay away from Annie. Instead, he shoved his hands in his pockets. "Haven't you hurt her enough?"

The elevator settled on the bottom floor with a slight rocking motion, then the doors opened. Together, the two men stepped out into the lobby. Grant carried his brother's suitcase, ready to toss him and his baggage on the streets of New York to fend for himself.

"I won't hurt her again."

"Yeah, right." Grant didn't want to hear any more. The thought of his brother pursuing Annie was obscene.

"I won't. I swear. I'm a changed man."

He faced his brother and shoved the bag into Griffin's arms. "Look, I'm tired of cleaning up your messes. I spent all day with that woman you abandoned. I like her. I wouldn't—"

"You like her?"

The truth of that statement rocked Grant. He released the bag in Griffin's hold and stepped back.

"Is that why she's staying with you? Are you *interested* in her? Are you putting the moves on her?" His voice rose with incredulity.

The truth shot through Grant and left a residual trail of guilt burning in his gut. "Thanks to you, she didn't have anywhere to go. She needed a place to stay. I thought it was the least I could do, seeing that you're my brother."

"Okay. Sorry." Griffin rubbed a hand across his forehead. "I didn't mean to accuse you of anything. Annie just makes me crazy. I guess it's love."

Grant wished he understood more about love so he could set Griffin straight on the subject.

His brother grinned at him. "So, will you help me?"

His insides twisted with indecision. Under no circumstances did he want to see Annie and Griffin together again. He knew he cared about her, wanted to protect her from being hurt, that's all. His brother was certainly the type to walk out and leave Annie, again.

But on the other hand, Grant couldn't pursue anything with her. She wanted things he didn't—couldn't—give. Hell, she wasn't for him. Maybe she'd actually be good for Griffin. Maybe if his brother settled down, he'd be forced to become responsible finally. Maybe Annie was right for him. For Griffin. Not for Grant.

Feeling his skin grow cold and a dull throb begin in his temple, he said, "All right."

# 8

GRANT AWOKE the next morning with a pounding headache. His spine felt twisted into tiny knots, his neck sore and stiff. It was closer to noon than dawn...not that he had anything planned.

Slowly, he sat up, stretching his arm along the back of the couch. Why had he fallen asleep here? What had he been celebrating? A bottle of champagne lay on its side, not a drop left. Maybe he'd been drowning his sorrows. He rubbed his temples. His brain felt sluggish. He couldn't think past the dull throbbing.

Pushing up from the couch, he traipsed to the bathroom. A hot shower would clear the fog from his mind, loosen the stiffness in his joints and erase the aches vibrating through his muscles.

Shrugging off his shirt, he tossed it behind him. He almost bumped his head against the closed door. What the hell? he thought. Confused, he twisted the knob and shoved open the door.

A startled gasp stopped him. His vision cleared instantly. His brain snapped on. Annie!

She stood in the middle of his bathroom. Her skin looked silky smooth, like the robe pooled at her feet. She grabbed the nearest towel and tried to cover herself. Unfortunately for her, and fortunately for him, it was a hand towel.

Slowly his gaze rose along her long, shapely legs.

They were lightly tanned. She wore a bikini of white flesh, her stomach golden to match her legs and arms. Her body had gentle curves and flat planes that he wanted to explore more thoroughly with his hands. But he couldn't move forward as his libido dictated or backward as a true gentleman should.

The hell with being a gentleman. Annie had teased his mind all night, tempting him with provocative kisses in his dreams. Now here she was in his bathroom. Naked!

His gaze fixated on her breasts. The morning chill in his apartment had puckered her nipples. He remembered the feel of them against his chest. He wanted to touch her now, kiss her, taste her skin. He took a step forward, the tile cold on his bare feet but his blood pumping liquid heat through his veins.

"Grant!" She looked as if the bottom hinge of her jaw had unlatched. Her disheveled hair curled and spiked about her head in an alluring manner. "What are you doing?"

Again, he stopped. What was he doing? What had he promised Griffin? Guilt pricked his conscience like tiny needles jabbing into his skin.

Damn. "I'm sorry, Annie. Um, I'm not used to company."

"It's okay," she said, her eyes still wide. "Just remember to knock next time."

"Right." Wrong. There wouldn't be a next time. He had to find her a place to stay—away from him and his overactive sex drive.

"Hi, Bert!" Annie smiled at the doorman as she raced to get out of Grant's apartment, to get her thoughts in order. Her face felt warm with a flush. She told herself it was her quick pace, not that Grant had seen her naked. "How are you doing this morning?"

"Fine, Mrs. Stevens." His greeting stopped her momentarily. With a rush, the last day poured through her mind, reminding her she wasn't really Mrs. Stevens. She was a fake one. "Going out on the town?"

"Yes indeed!" she said, focusing on her new plan to experience all life had to offer. "I've never been to New York."

"Well, then be sure and see all the attractions."

Attractions? Annie needed a distraction from the main attraction in Grant's apartment. Her preoccupation with Grant and his well-muscled physique was too much.

"Wait up, Annie!" Grant called, jogging up behind her. "What's the hurry?"

She shrugged and tilted her chin back so she could see the sky. "It's a beautiful day!"

"Uh-huh."

"And I don't want to waste a minute." Actually she didn't want to stay cooped up with Grant and think about the morning's embarrassment in the bathroom. A tingle rippled through her abdomen.

Twice now he'd seen her without clothes. Okay, once in the altogether. And once almost, with her underwear barely covering her. The memory made her skin flush. If only she could see him naked. Just to even the score, she thought with a secretive smile.

"I'm excited to begin my new life is all," she said, rushing out onto the sidewalk.

Horns blared and people rushed passed. She took a semi-deep breath but almost choked on the strange, exotic smells. Hot dogs, exhaust fumes, some peculiar Oriental spice...and things she didn't want to overanalyze. She tilted back her head and squinted up at the reflection of the sun glinting off some twenty-story building. This definitely wasn't Lockett.

"Looks like everyone's in a hurry this morning. I should fit right in. I guess they aren't rushing off to Sunday school, huh?"

"Doubtful." He gave her a wry smile.

Her gaze shifted, locking on to a man who was staring at her. He wore an overcoat, even though the sun was warm, the breeze mild. She nodded and said, "Hiya."

"Don't do that," Grant scolded, his tone similar to her own when she reprimanded one of her students. He clasped her elbow in a firm grip and steered her into the steady flow of traffic.

Her hackles raised, she snapped at him. "What?"

"Didn't anybody ever tell you not to talk to strangers?"

She blinked at his coldness. "What are you? Still playing my husband, or have you switched to my father now?"

He kept his hand on her elbow as if to jerk her back if she went astray. "It's not safe to talk to people on the streets here. This isn't west Texas where cows and tumbleweed outnumber people. You don't know these people. You don't know if you just said hello to a psychopath or not."

"Oh, Grant, you watch too much late-night TV."

"I watch the news. It's not fiction." He shook his head and frowned. "Strange people live here."

"Like you?" she asked, tossing the remark over her

shoulder and speeding ahead of him. Her stomach rumbling, she aimed for the vendor on the corner.

Grant caught up with her and grabbed her hand.

She glanced down at their entwined fingers, which seemed to link together naturally. A shuddering awareness rocked through her and she pulled her hand away. "What are you doing?"

"If you're hungry then you have to have a New York breakfast. Not a hot dog."

Remembering Griff's warning yesterday gave her pause. "You think I eat too much?"

"What?"

"Do I eat too much...too much junk food?"

"Turn around," Grant said with a mischievous grin.

"No."

He shrugged, then took her elbow. She pulled back in a pretend tug-of-war.

"You didn't answer me."

"Because the question is absurd. Look at you! Maybe every woman in New York should start eating hot dogs, chocolate and caramel parfaits and five slices of pizza."

"You counted how much pizza I ate?"

"Annie," he said, his voice warm and engaging, "I watch everything about you with amazement. Now, come on, let's eat. I'm hungry."

His words made her skin tingle. She wondered what exactly he was hungry for. "If you're talking a bagel and cream cheese, then point me in the right direction."

He smiled and tilted his head to the right. She saw the green-striped canopy over a door. The tiny deli-market was smashed between a Starbucks and a Ben & Jerry's. Mmm, dessert! "Do they have lox?"

His upper lip curled. "If you really want it."

"I want to try everything!"

"Okay, then." He waved her through the door first then followed her inside. "Here we go."

"Do you eat here often?"

"Sometimes." He picked up an orange, tossed it up in the air, then caught it. "Depends."

"On what?"

"If I have an early-morning meeting or not."

They stepped behind a small elderly woman who held her purse against her stomach. The line was short, but while they waited Annie digested the things around her. Plump grapes from Israel. Juicy peaches from Georgia. Ripe cantaloupe halves and honeydew melons from somewhere she'd never heard of. There was a long salad bar set up toward the back. Along each wall were stacked rows and rows of groceries. Cereal, diapers, spices. It sure wasn't the Piggly Wiggly back in Lockett. This had an exotic feel, an energy that she found intoxicating. But...the prices! Oh my! How would she ever afford living here?

"Coffee?" Grant asked.

"Leaded."

"Sugar?"

"Of course. Cream, too."

He grinned. "I should have known."

"One day of marriage and you think you know me so well," she joked. The lady in front of them turned, cocked a faded eyebrow at them then turned back around to place her order.

"I just know you're not one to run from a few calories," Grant teased.

"Does it show?" she asked, then wished she'd kept her mouth shut.

His gaze skimmed down her body like a slow caress. Heat seared her cheeks. She knew he wasn't seeing her T-shirt and jeans but what was underneath—which was bare skin. She certainly wasn't wearing that uncomfortable pushup bra from yesterday, nor that garter and stockings.

"Not a bit." He rubbed his jaw. "But then again, maybe I ought to take another look."

Her brain turned to oatmeal, her knees to Jell-O. What was wrong with her? She was usually more levelheaded about men. Or was she? After all, she should have learned her lesson from three failed engagements. She shouldn't be reacting to him like this. But the fact was she'd never reacted to anyone this way before.

Before she could think of a reply to his invitation, she heard her name. She looked toward the front of the deli and saw Griffin walk through the open door.

"Morning all!" He waved at them.

"Griffin?" she asked. "What are you doing here?"

"Grant called, said you two might be going sightseeing."

"Oh." She shifted her gaze toward Grant. "You called Griff?"

He coughed. "Well, I, uh, thought..."

"You don't mind if I come along for the tour, do you?" Griffin asked.

Still staring at Grant, she wondered if he didn't want to be alone with her. Was he trying to avoid her?

Did he want to get rid of her? That thought was like a slash to her heart. What should it matter what Grant thought of her? Why should it matter if he wanted to get rid of her? But it did. Oh, it did!

"Not at all," she said, avoiding the dull ache in her heart. "Come along."

"Good. I haven't spent much time in New York. Should have come more often to visit my big brother."

"Family's important," she said in a distracted tone.

She had a hard time seeing the two men growing up together. Griffin had always acted more small town, even in his sales job of selling special fertilizers to farmers. Maybe that's why he'd been successful. Their similar upbringing in small-town America had connected them, made her feel as if they'd known each other their whole lives.

But Grant made her feel...not comfortable. But not uncomfortable. Something in between. Something different, unusual, indescribable.

Griffin and Grant had both wanted to escape their small hometown in Oklahoma. But that's where their similarities ended. Griffin had gone to Dallas and started selling manure, not necessarily a far stretch. Grant had headed for New York and Wall Street.

Dressed in his casual jeans, boat shoes and loose-knit shirt, Grant looked as if he belonged here. He had a sophisticated, cosmopolitan quality, a debonair confidence that was more refined than Griffin's looming ego.

Frankly, placing the two brothers side by side, Griffin came in a distant second to Grant's calm demeanor and almost overwhelming sexiness. In some ways Grant intimidated her, unraveled her nerves. He seemed to know so much more than she did. He had so much more experience. He had a high-powered job and lived in The City. He knew if he liked lox or not, while she had so much to learn. At the same time, he made her feel safe, protected.

Forcing herself to look at Griffin, to keep her mind off Grant, she wondered if she'd ever really known her ex-fiancé at all.

"Here we go," Grant said, taking a white paper sack full of bagels from the clerk. He handed Annie a plastic cup of coffee. "Do you want to eat here or on the go?"

"On the go is fine," she said, her mouth beginning to water at the smell of yeast rising out of the sack.

Griffin dug in the sack and gave everyone a wrapped bagel, the cream cheese slathered and melting between the warm, toasted sides. "Where are we going? Ellis Island? Statue of Liberty?"

Grant laughed. "I bet we don't get farther than the corner today."

His brother frowned at him. "Why?"

Annie smiled, knowing exactly what Grant was thinking. He'd only known her a day and already he knew her fairly well, already he knew she was imagining sampling the ice cream next door. "Because of me."

"What's wrong? Can't you walk?" Her ex-fiancé's gaze skimmed over her.

She waited for that physical jolt, a trailing shimmy of excitement, but she felt nothing. Had she grown immune to Griff's looks, his kisses? In just one day?

With a sly wink that they'd keep Griffin in the dark about her penchant for food, any kind of food, Grant touched her elbow and escorted her out the door. "I thought we'd head to Times Square. Maybe see if there's a show Annie might want to see later in the week."

"Annie, how long are you going to stay in New York?"

"I told you last night, Griff, I don't know."

"But..." Griffin seemed to mull this over. "I just thought you were miffed at me. Don't you want to go home...at least to Texas?"

"Not yet. Maybe not ever."

"Here," Grant said, catching a break in the traffic to cross the street. "Come on."

"Anybody want to know what I want to see?" Griffin called after them, getting left behind in order to avoid being hit by a speeding taxi.

Annie forgot about her ex-fiancé the second Grant put his hand on her waist to guide her across the street.

"WHY DID YOU move here?" Annie asked over a corned beef sandwich the size of a small steer.

Grant shrugged. "This is where you have to be for investment banking."

"And do you like it?" she asked, ignoring Griffin's pout. As the day wore on, his shoulders had become hunched from frustration, or irritation; she wasn't sure which, nor did she care.

"Mostly. Sometimes I miss home. The wide-open spaces. The breathable air. The sunshine."

"The cow manure?" Griffin asked sarcastically.

"Not when I've got you, the manure salesman." Grant laughed.

Griffin scowled.

"What made you want to be an investment banker?" Annie asked, still comparing the two brothers.

"It was expected," Griffin answered for him. "We were forced to go to college."

"Meet the true rebel without a cause," Grant said.

"Damn straight. And I've done fine without a degree."

Grant nodded his agreement. Annie could see him working something over in his mind but he kept it to himself. He swallowed a bite of his Philly cheese steak sandwich.

"Mom and Dad simply wanted the best for us," Grant said. "They were proud of our abilities and wanted us to go as far as we could. They worked hard, scrimping and saving pennies so we could go to school. They made sure we were given more opportunities than they were. I took advantage of it."

"You took a scholarship," Griff replied, shoving a french fry into his mouth, "which really put the pressure on me."

"Gave you more of Mom and Dad's money to blow," Grant said, "which you did."

Griffin rolled his eyes. "Sometimes you have to live by instinct, by the seat of your pants. Just go for it."

"Maybe you should go into advertising," Grant said.

"What's that supposed to mean?" Griffin asked, the chip on his shoulder growing by the minute.

Annie hid a smile. Grant made her laugh. He made her feel things. Too many things.

She glued her attention to Griffin, where it was safer. She had always wanted to be footloose and fancy free, gutsy, travel on a whim, skip town in a heartbeat. But her parents' illnesses, then other responsibilities, had kept her in Lockett much longer than she would have liked. Listening to her ex-fiancé made her reevaluate her desires.

Wanting to explore her thoughts, wanting to draw a definite line between her dreams and Griffin's reality, she said, "Is that philosophy what made you go off and leave me waiting at the altar?"

"Annie—" He reached for her.

She moved her hand, grabbed her fork and jabbed it into the coleslaw.

"Did you decide which show you'd like to see?" Grant asked, abruptly changing the topic.

Appreciating his sensitivity, she said, "Yeah, I think I'd like to see *Swing*."

"Good choice," he said. "After lunch we'll get in line."

She glanced across the street at Times Square. She'd started to think she'd never see famous places like this for herself. Already today, she'd seen Grand Central Station, Carnegie Hall and, of course, Macy's.

"Then what?" she asked.

"You seemed interested in the Empire State Building as we drove into the city. Why don't we go to the top?"

Grant's thoughtfulness touched her. When had Griffin or any of her other fiancés ever acquiesced to her wishes? Never. And she knew then she'd never settle for less again.

OVER THE COURSE of the afternoon, as they wandered through bookstores and meandered along the streets of New York City, she saw her ex-fiancé in a new way. Why had she ever wanted to marry him, much less thought it a good idea?

What troubled her most was the bridge that had formed between Grant and her. A friendship had begun, but it felt shaky, unstable, as if it could come tumbling down at any moment. She felt unsure and unsteady around him. Not so much because of him, but because of the strange feelings she was having for him. Griffin, however, seemed safer, less risky.

Walking briskly between the two men as they traipsed through the lobby of the Empire State Building, she noticed evening shades of amber bouncing off the marble. She realized she'd loved Griffin—and Rodney and Travis—as selfishly as they had loved themselves. In the end, their fears had driven them away from her before she'd made a terrible mistake, before she'd realized her own error. She'd wanted what they had to offer—a ticket out of Lockett.

Realizing her own selfishness struck a painful chord inside her. She'd loved three men. But not truly, not in the way one should love for all eternity. Yet at the same time, the conscious understanding of her motives settled her nerves. At least she now knew she could make the move on her own, without anyone's help, without marrying someone. Thankfully, she wasn't as flighty as she'd once thought, easily falling in and out of love.

But it still didn't explain the strange feelings she had for Grant. Determined to resist the pull toward him, she looped her arm through Griffin's as they boarded the elevator that would take them up eighty-six flights.

"Have you ever been up here?" she asked.

"Nope." Griffin pressed her arm against the side of his chest as if it was natural for her to want to be near him. As if nothing had changed between them. "You, Grant?"

"Occasionally."

Suddenly, Annie knew why Griffin had joined them today. He thought he could get her back. Why he wanted her now, she couldn't figure out, but she knew without a doubt that she didn't want him.

She wanted Grant.

*No, no, no! It's too soon. He's too...risky.*

She'd survived three broken engagements only because she realized now that she'd never given her heart totally to any of her fiancés. But Grant would be different.

No, he wouldn't. He was not the settling-down type. Therefore, he was off-limits. That was why she felt safer with Griffin. She wasn't about to make a mistake with him again.

She thought of *An Affair to Remember*. The characters had a sacrificial kind of love, a love that sought to protect the other. Yet at the same time it was a love that was prideful and selfish, that protected them from rejection. *They were characters, Annie. They weren't real.*

"What is it with women?" Grant asked, watching them from across the elevator with a heavy-lidded gaze. "Why do they always want to come here?"

"It's romantic," she said, feeling the confident heat from Griffin press against her yet feeling nothing for him in return.

"It's a building," Grant countered.

"It's the movie," Griffin explained. "You know that one...what was it?" He snapped his fingers. "*Sleepless in Seattle.*"

"*An Affair to Remember.*" Annie rolled her eyes.

"Never heard of it," Grant said.

"Chick flick," Griff explained.

Annie rolled her eyes.

"Is that the one Tom Hanks was sobbing over in *Sleepless*—"

"Nah," Griff interrupted. "That was *The Dirty Dozen.*"

Grant gave his brother a quizzical look. "Doesn't sound sappy. But I haven't seen that one, either."

Griff laughed and slipped his arm around Annie's waist. "He doesn't get out much, as you can tell."

Grant ignored them but she had a feeling he understood exactly what they were talking about. He was the type to avoid romance at all costs. And she'd do well to remember that.

# 9

GRANT CAUGHT the look. It was the slight tilt of his brother's head that said, "Get the hell out of here." As soon as they stepped off the elevator at the top of the Empire State Building and walked out onto the observation deck, he made himself scarce.

A warm summer breeze poured over him, ruffling his hair, whipping at his jacket. His gaze scanned the panoramic view of Manhattan. The glittering top of the Chrysler Building attracted his attention momentarily.

Then he noticed all the couples walking around the observation deck hand in hand. Immediately his gaze snapped back to Annie. He couldn't stop watching her, noticing every nuance, each curve, and wondering what she was saying to Griffin. He wanted to be with Annie himself, without his brother's intrusive presence. Why the hell had he called Griffin to meet them that morning anyway?

Because he'd made a promise.

Damn.

They sauntered away from him, Griffin's arm snug around Annie's waist, leading her toward a spot where they could see the East River. Grant felt a pinch of irritation. Or was it jealousy? That would be a first. He'd never been jealous over a woman. Never coveted what a friend or co-worker had. Never envied his brother, either. Never wanted anything Griffin had acquired...except Annie. And he couldn't have her.

He jammed his hands in his pockets, felt a chill rip through him and stared down at the little rectangular patch known as Central Park. He heard her laughter and felt a piece of himself plummet like a coin thrown over the edge of the building.

How did Griffin do it? First he romanced her. Then he dumped her. And now he was winning her back!

Anger shot through Grant. He took two steps toward them, then stopped, his hands balled into fists, his breathing harsh. He wanted to tell Annie how irresponsible Griffin was. He wanted to tell her Griffin was all wrong for her. He wanted to say she could have any man she wanted. She could have... Who? Grant?

No.

He didn't want marriage. He didn't want Annie. At least, not permanently.

He'd known her for less than two days. But those forty-eight hours had been jam-packed with raw emotions. It was the kind of time where you could learn a lot about someone, what made them tick, what ticked them off. He'd marveled at her energy and optimism. Her enthusiasm as she explored New York was both contagious and unnerving. It had been almost ten years since he'd moved here from Oklahoma and he'd forgotten how he'd felt when he'd arrived—scared, inspired, charged. Yet, as a transplanted southerner turned jaded New Yorker, he knew the dangers she could face if she wasn't careful. His need to protect her unraveled him.

He'd never wanted to take care of someone. Oh, he had though. He'd done his duty as a son, helping his folks on the ranch during his younger years before he'd moved off. Then when his father passed away, he'd sent his mother money, helped her with the often confusing world of finances and insurance that she'd never bothered with, called her each week and visited as often as possible. When she'd become sick, he'd gone home for several weeks until the end. He'd also tried to look after his little brother. The weight of responsibility had always been heavy on him. But he hadn't minded. He certainly wasn't a saint by any stretch of the imagination. He was simply a man.

A man who wanted a woman. And that woman was Annie.

Griffin turned Annie toward him. The humor between them evaporated, and their expressions, highlighted by the emerging starlight, turned serious, as if they were taking their vows together here on the top of the Empire State Building. Annie had said it was a romantic spot. He didn't get it. Fact was, he was about to get ill.

Crossing his arms over his chest, he backed away, still unable to look away. If she wanted to mess up her life, then it was hers to do so. If she wanted to make a colossal mistake with Griffin, then who was he to stop her? What did he care anyway?

*Fine, go ahead, Annie. Marry my brother.*

Griffin pulled her close. Annie raised up on tiptoe and kissed him. *She* kissed *him!* Grant flinched as if he'd been struck. Then he turned away. Why was he torturing himself with something he couldn't have?

IT WAS A SIMPLE, chaste, heartfelt kiss of goodbye, then Annie wriggled out of Griffin's embrace. "Thank you for understanding."

He pinched his lips together, forming two parentheses on either side of his mouth. "Are you sure about this?"

She nodded. A chill settled into her bones and she chafed her arms. It was breezier on top of the Empire State Building than she'd imagined. Maybe because she'd always thought of it in a romantic way. Or maybe she hadn't thought about it logically. Like so many things in her life.

"Okay then," Griff said, apparently not crushed by her emphatic refusal of his latest marriage proposal. "Let's go find my big brother."

Exactly what she wanted to do anyway.

Her gaze ping-ponged around the observation deck. She saw families with overwrought parents and little kids running circles around them or running them in circles. Couples smooched and cuddled in darkening shadows, possibly creating their own affair to remember. A few individuals gazed out at the spectacular view, perhaps making wishes on the brightening stars. But Grant was nowhere to be seen.

"Where'd he go anyway?" she asked, ignoring the jab of disappointment.

"Maybe he went back to the lobby," Griffin said after they'd circled the deck once.

"I wonder why," she said.

"It's a guy thing."

Giving him a curious glance, she entered the crowded elevator. On the drop down, she felt her stomach fall at a slower pace, then rush to catch up with the rest of her as the doors slid open.

"There he is," Griffin said as they stepped off the elevator. "Where'd you go, Grant?"

With his hands jammed in his jacket pockets, his hair ruffled in a sexy way that she shouldn't be noticing, Grant scowled. "I thought that was obvious."

His sarcasm grabbed her attention. "Is something wrong, Grant?"

"No. Are y'all through here?"

"Yeah. We're through all right." Griffin rubbed the back of his neck. "Look, Grant, would you, uh, mind seeing Annie back to your place. I've got some calls to make. I don't want to waste my time here in New York."

Annie ignored the tiny jabs he made in her direction. She had nothing to feel guilty about. "Business calls," Grant said without an ounce of derision.

"Take care of my girl. Okay?"

"Yeah," Grant said, completing the handoff.

Annie felt like a tossed football. Her ego tousled, she squared her shoulders. She could take care of herself. She wasn't a child, someone to be baby-sat. What was it with these men?

Grant's gaze shifted toward her then, pierced her with his intense scrutiny and quashed her snap defense. There was understanding in the depths of his eyes, a tenderness that made her feel suddenly weak, as if she did need someone bigger, braver and stronger to look after her.

Before she could contemplate and sort through her feelings, Griffin leaned toward her, pressed a kiss to her cheek and whispered, "Bye, darlin'."

But she wasn't really listening. Her gaze remained on Grant. He looked discreetly away, turning even his shoulder toward them.

"Bye, Griff." She watched her ex-fiancé walk out of her life. She'd wondered how she'd feel when this moment arrived. Now she knew. She felt free, like a bird soaring over the clouds.

"You okay?" Grant asked, studying her again.

"Cold." She wrapped her arms across her middle as the coolness of the evening settled back around her.

"Here." He shrugged out of his jacket and placed it around her shoulders, his hands gently pushing her hair out of the way.

His touch made her scalp tingle. The lining of his jacket felt soft, like brushed cotton, and was warm with his body heat and tinged with his seductive scent. She snuggled inside it, pulling the front flaps together with her fist. "Thanks."

Putting a hand to her back, he led her away from the Empire State Building. They walked side by side, their hands almost touching but not quite. It gave her an unsettled, restless, antsy feeling.

"Hungry?" he asked.

She slanted her gaze toward him. "I thought you knew me better than to ask that."

His mouth pulled into a lopsided grin. "A woman with a real appetite. What are you in the mood for?"

*You.*

She gave herself a mental shake. Yes, she was attracted to Grant. But she was not ready to jump into another relationship. Not now. Maybe not ever.

Realizing he was waiting for an answer, she finally said, "Your choice."

"I know a great little Italian place." He indicated with his hand to cross the street. "It's not far if you're game to walk."

At her conceding nod, they raced across the congested street, dodging taxis, hurdling the curb in the middle and bobbing around a group of Japanese tourists. Catching her breath, Annie said, "I thought you said walk."

Grant laughed and slowed his steps. They fell into a comfortable pace. Neon lights and car horns vied for her attention. But Grant held it securely. She was aware of every inch of him—his broad shoulders, his long legs with their purposeful stride, his hands so close, so gentle, so strong.

"I guess you've been to the observation deck before," she said, unnerved by her obsession with Grant. Shouldn't she be mourning her loss of Griffin? But how could she, when all she felt was relief?

"A couple of times."

"Griff said guys aren't interested in sight-seeing. That it isn't a guy thing."

Grant shrugged. "I think he meant it's not a romantic spot like you'd said earlier."

"Oh? And what is your idea of a romantic spot?" she challenged him.

He stopped suddenly, yanked on her elbow and pulled her close. If they both took a deep breath, her breasts would have touched his chest. Her insides warmed with the idea of him kissing her. She lifted her chin, expectant, hopeful.

But then something jarred her from behind and she fell into Grant. He steadied her, his arms coming around her. When she looked up at him, he was staring over her head, frowning at someone who'd raced past them, his look stern, disapproving.

"Are you okay?" he asked, his attention shifting to her.

"Yes." No. Not if he didn't kiss her.

"Sorry about that." He loosened his hold but didn't release her completely. "I saw that jerk about to collide with you."

"Oh," was all she could manage. "Uh, what were you saying about..." She couldn't think with him so near.

"Romance?" His fingers closed over her upper arm, sending tiny rivulets of desire pouring through her and pooling in her middle. "The place doesn't matter. It can happen anywhere," he said, his voice slow and reflective, "if it's the right person. You don't need heights or starlight or any of that peripheral stuff."

Her throat felt tight with anticipation. "What do you need?" Me? she hoped. "For romance, that is."

"A kiss. Here." He brushed his thumb across the bottom of her lip. "And here." His hand slid along her jaw and settled along the curve of her neck. "Soft music is nice. Something like...Vivaldi or even Jim Brickman. Hell, I guess you could have Kiss making the windows rattle from the noise and it wouldn't matter. Depends on the couple. The man, the woman..."

She was staring at his mouth, wishing he'd kiss her again. Her skin felt hot, flushed.

"This is it."

"Yes," she breathed, believing even this busy intersection in the middle of downtown Manhattan could be romantic. With Grant.

"The restaurant," he said, tipping his head to the building beside them.

The moment stretched until she snapped to attention with understanding. "Oh! The restaurant." Her gaze slid up the brick building to the awning above the entrance. Some Italian word, she guessed, was highlighted with lights. "Right. Good. Well, okay, uh, let's go inside."

He stepped away first. Her knees felt unsteady, her heartbeat erratic. He held the door open for her to enter the dark restaurant. There was a crowd waiting for tables and they had to stand near the entrance, forced as close as two lovers would stand. The zesty aromas of oregano and garlic made her mouth water instantly. But the feel of Grant pressed close to her made her feel things...want things...need things. Need him. Her stomach felt as if it was melting. Her heart pounded as though it might leap out of her chest at any minute. A trembling started deep inside her and spread to her limbs.

"You still cold?" Grant asked.

"I'm fine." She hugged his jacket tighter and dipped her chin into the V-neck opening. She smelled his musky cologne and a tickle of desire rippled through her abdomen and spread along her spine.

"It'll be a short wait. Is that okay?"

"Sure. Whatever." She secretly hoped it would take a long time for the maître d' to find a table. She wasn't necessarily proud of her bold reaction to Grant, but she couldn't deny it, either.

"So," he said, his mouth close to her ear so she could hear him over the din of conversations surrounding them, "what are your plans for tomorrow?"

"I was thinking of looking for a job."

He pulled back an inch. "Here? In New York?"

She nodded. "I like it here. I want to test the waters."

"See if you're going to sink or swim?"

"So to speak."

It became difficult to carry on a conversation, trying to compete with the boisterous voices around them and the piped-in violin music. She looked out the window across the street at the triple-X movie house, the family deli next door and next to that an aromatherapy center. She watched the people walk by on the street. Those alone walked with their gazes down, up or fixed straight head and never let their gaze drift toward a passerby. Some sauntered in pairs, hands clasped, hips swaying in a side-by-side fashion that hinted of intimacy. Some looked as if they were in training for the Olympics, arms pumping, breaths coming hard and fast.

She'd always thought New York was chic, cosmopolitan, but in reality the people, despite their fast-paced lives, had a casual attitude and dress that appealed to her. She'd seen women in linen suits wearing Nike tennis shoes and carrying handbags the size of a suitcase. Never would someone in Lockett have been caught in a fancy dress with shoes and a purse that didn't match. Maybe her hometown, although laid-back and intimate, was more formal, more pretentious, than New York. Maybe that's why she'd always figured she had to get married.

But why? Why couldn't she be casual about life, the way people in New York seemed to be? Why did she have to be so intense? So serious?

Being attracted to Grant didn't mean she had to

have a serious relationship with him. It could be casual. Temporary. Hot.

She breathed in his scent and imagined them together, bodies pressing closer, mouths joined. It was definitely something to consider.

But she knew, just as the restaurant had been Grant's choice, this was her move. But did she dare take it?

"What about Griffin?" Grant practically yelled, but because of the noise she could barely hear him. "Is that what he's doing tonight? Looking for a way to move here, too?"

She frowned. "Why would he do that?"

"To be near you. Isn't that what most couples do?"

"What?"

"Try to be together!" he emphasized each word.

She shook her head. She hadn't heard him right. Was Grant saying he wanted to be together? With her? Her heart kicked up the beat.

"Or are y'all going to be bicoastal?"

Y'all? Her hope deflated. He meant Griffin. Would Griffin always be between them? So that's it, she thought. That's why Grant had left them alone on the observation deck. But was it why, when they'd found him in the lobby, he'd been cranky as a startled rattlesnake? Hope—or maybe a small case of insanity—swelled inside her, clouding her judgment. She couldn't stifle the secretive smile that tugged at her lips. "We're not going to be anything."

"What did you say?"

"We're through," she yelled, desperate to make him understand that nothing, nobody, stood between them anymore.

"What?"

"We're over!"

Suddenly the restaurant went silent. Heads turned. Eyes focused on her, especially Grant's gaze. She flushed.

"Uh," she said, "we're over. Griffin and I."

"Over?" Grant asked.

"It's over," somebody with a thick New York accent said. "Okay? *O-V-E-R*. Need her to say it again?"

# 10

THE END. *Kaput. Hasta la vista*, Griffin!

A self-satisfied smile spread across Grant's face as reality sunk in. So, his younger brother was now out of the picture. Good.

To hide his pleasure, he took a sip of his wine. The soft, balanced Merlot slid down his throat. With her fork, Annie jabbed at a tomato lying in a bed of lettuce. He watched her slip the plump vegetable into her mouth, the juice moistening her lips, making him uncomfortable. After two glasses of wine he felt a warmth flow through him, but instead of blurring his senses the drink had sharpened his thoughts.

What was he thinking? That now Annie was available? Good God, she'd just been dumped! By his brother! She needed some time before she sprang back and entered another relationship. Didn't she?

Not that he wanted a relationship.

But he did want *her*—bad. More than he'd ever wanted any woman. And he'd wanted plenty. But not now. Now he simply wanted Annie.

He tried to tell himself it was her vivid blue eyes, her silky skin, luscious mouth...curvaceous body. Hell, he knew it was more. It was all of her. The whole package. And it was the whole package that scared him.

When she finished her linguini, she wore a satisfied

look, her eyes full, her lips parted slightly. He wondered if he could satisfy her another way. He stared at
a burgundy spot of wine on the white linen tablecloth.
He dabbed at it with his finger and thought of how intoxicating Annie's kisses were. Damn.

He shifted in his seat. He could feel the faint heat
from the candle in the middle of the table. A tiny wisp
of smoke rose and vanished, soaked up by the aromas
of Italian food. He remembered the heat Annie's body
generated when she pressed against him. What the
hell was wrong with him?

She was a woman. Just like any other woman he'd
ever known. He could take his pleasure, enjoy her as
she could enjoy him, and that would be all. The end.

But for some reason, with Annie, he knew it would
be different.

*Run!* his mind warned. But he couldn't. Dammit, he
didn't want to.

"I'm as full as a tick on a dog's behind," she said.

He laughed. Okay, she wasn't like any woman he'd
ever known.

He liked her sense of humor, her colloquial sayings,
her optimism, almost better than her kiss. Was that
humanly possible? "Better not let anybody hear you
say that in this town. They'll know you're not a Yan-
kee."

Folding her napkin and placing it in the empty spot
her plate had occupied, she grinned. "All I have to do
is open my mouth. My Texas drawl runs deep."

So did his feelings for her, which shocked him. They
hadn't known each other long enough for love to de-
velop.

He thought of the women he'd dated who'd pressed

for a commitment. He'd never felt this way about any of them, not even Susan. He realized now that their combustible relationship had been like a fuse on a powder keg. Once blown, there wasn't anything left. Except devastation, if he didn't handle her very carefully.

Susan had a quick New York temper. He didn't want to get on the wrong side of it, not before he'd taken her company public. He couldn't afford to lose her account now. And Annie could definitely jeopardize everything, especially if Susan thought he'd dumped her for Annie.

"So where are you going to look for a teaching job?" he asked, trying to keep his mind coherent, away from thoughts of a relationship with Annie.

"First I have to find out the requirements for getting my accreditation in New York. Then I'll probably apply at some private schools. They are usually more lenient and will often help you get accreditation."

"Sounds like a plan."

"Grant, I know what you're really asking," she said, leaning forward. Her fingers grazed his hand, paralyzing him.

"What?" Could she see how much he wanted her? What the hell had he said?

"I promise I won't inconvenience you for long."

"Annie—"

"It's okay. I understand. My mother always taught me not to wear out my welcome. I'm going to look into new accommodations tomorrow, too."

"Why?"

Her laughter sputtered. "Haven't I been enough trouble to you already?"

"You haven't been any trouble." Griffin had.

"Oh, yeah! I just forced you to marry me, ended up flying here with you, then camped out in your apartment."

"It's no trouble." But his feelings for her were definitely troublesome.

"Look, Grant, you don't have to worry about me."

"I'm not." *I'm worried about myself. Good God, what am I thinking about?*

"You don't have to help me out of loyalty to your brother, either."

"I'm not." He *wanted* to help her. He *needed* to be with her.

"Then why?" she asked. "Why are you doing this?"

*If only he knew.* He couldn't decipher his feelings. It wasn't purely altruistic. Maybe it was wholly selfish. No, it was more than that. He simply couldn't let her go off on her own yet.

But he'd have to soon, for her own benefit as well as his own.

"Let's just say I want to help. Not for Griffin. Not out of guilt. Not for any other reason but..." his gaze met hers and a warmth filled him "...for you."

A fragile thread of spun glass formed between them. One breath, one hasty word, one wrong move, and it would be broken.

He had to watch himself. He didn't want to scare her or chase her off. He had to treat her as he would a wounded animal.

"Dessert?" the waitress said, the air still vibrating between them.

"No," Annie said in a whisper-soft voice, not looking away from Grant, her gaze magnetizing him. "I'm not hungry."

But her eyes said her hunger matched his own.

*IT'S NOW OR NEVER*, Annie thought as they entered his apartment a little while later.

*Don't do it*, one side of her brain warned.

*Oh, go for it!* the other side encouraged. *After all, what do you have to lose?*

*Your heart*, the other side spoke up again.

Her insides trembled with uncertainty. What should she do? Play by the rules? Look where that had gotten her. No, this was not a time to waffle. This was her new life. It could be anything she wanted it to be.

But... What would Grant do? He had a mind of his own. Would he turn her away? Would he say he wasn't interested?

She couldn't believe she was planning a seduction. Well, it was better than a wedding. At least if he turned her away it wouldn't be in front of the hometown crowd. But, for some reason, she knew it would be even more painful.

"Thanks for the use of your jacket," she said, slipping it from her shoulders.

"You're welcome." His features looked as hard as granite in the dim lighting. Shadows deepened the contours of his face, shaded his eyes. If only she could tell what he was thinking. If only she had a crystal ball and could see in it exactly what Grant's reaction would be.

"Grant—"

"Annie—"

They spoke at the same time, then they both fell silent. An unnerving stillness vibrated through the spacious room. She could hear the whir of traffic several stories below, the tick of a clock across the room, the hum of the air conditioner.

"I, uh..." She spoke to fill the void. But how could she explain her feelings, her needs, her desire?

"Go ahead," he encouraged her.

"I don't want Griffin," she blurted the words out into the open.

Grant stared at her, confusion darkening his brow. "O-kay. What do you want?"

Who? was a better question. But she couldn't say, "You."

Or could she?

What would a native New Yorker do? A woman who lived here would probably be suave, sophisticated. Maybe she'd puff a cigarette, exhale elegantly and sashay toward the bedroom, leaving a trail of smoke as an invitation. But Annie couldn't see herself doing that. She'd just choke and wheeze on the smoke. And besides, she couldn't see Grant interested in someone who smoked. Maybe a confident New Yorker would simply be blunt, put her cards right on the table. Suddenly, Annie felt inexperienced, naive, ridiculous. She didn't belong here. She wanted to go back home.

No, she didn't.

"I don't want to go home to Texas, either." What was she saying? She was doing everything wrong. But what was the right way to seduce your ex-fiancé's brother? Where was Emily Post when she needed her?

"I thought we settled that. You can stay here for as

long as you want." He watched her closely, judging to see if she'd suddenly lost her mind. "Are you okay?"

Maybe she was thinking too much. Maybe she should just follow her gut instincts.

She swallowed the hard lump in her throat and closed the gap between them. She touched a button on his shirt, felt his quick intake of breath, the contraction of the muscles embracing his ribs. "Grant?"

"Yes?" His voice sounded compressed.

Raising on tiptoe, she met his gaze briefly and felt the impact clear down to her toes. Her stomach rippled with awareness, uncertainty, hope. *Oh, God! Here I go. For better or worse.*

Squeezing her eyes shut, she slanted her mouth across his and kissed him, just like that.

Stunned by her own actions, she felt nothing for a moment. Then she felt the warmth, the generosity of his lips. It took her a moment to realize he hadn't pushed her away, but he hadn't grabbed her close and bent her backward in a knee-dipping, head-swooning kiss, either. What were they going to do? Just stand here, their mouths pressed together...forever?

To gauge the situation and his response better, she opened one eye. He stared back at her. He remained still and unmoving as if waiting for her.

"Annie," he said against her mouth, "do you know what you're doing?"

"Y-yes. I'm kissing you." Why did this one feel more awkward than the others they'd shared? What had she done wrong? She started to pull away.

But his hands settled on her waist and he gave her a toe-curling smile. "Good. That's what I thought. Now, kiss me like you mean it."

Her pulse jump-started. She closed her eyes and threw herself into the kiss, wrapping her arms around Grant's neck for support.

He kissed her back with the same ardor, the same greediness, the same raw hunger. His mouth conformed to hers, accommodating, taking, transforming her into a new creature. Touch and texture blended, blurred. Her mind reeled.

Then her hand closed in a fist. She grasped a wad of his shirt, pulled him closer, needing him, wanting him, the ache in her so powerful. She needed more, needed it now. And that scared her.

She broke away to take a much-needed breath. She felt dizzy with the heat. "I want you, Grant. Here. Now."

His fingers slid through her hair, and he sandwiched her head between his hands, gently, sweetly. He spoke no words but, rather, used touches and kisses that dissolved the last of her reservations. He kissed along the curve of her neck and slant of her shoulder, nibbling at her flesh, driving her wild. She felt his breath, warm and moist, on her skin. Something inside her opened and she knew only Grant could fill that empty wanting.

She released a shuddering breath. "I'm not looking for romance. Okay?"

"Fine," he growled.

Her fingers dug into his shoulders. *Don't stop*, she wanted to say, *what your tongue is doing to my ear*. Instead, she said with a breathy voice, "I don't want a relationship, either."

"Annie." He cupped her jaw and whispered against her mouth, "Shut up." Then his mouth took hers with a savage need that frightened, overwhelmed and aroused her.

The next thing she knew, her back was pressed against the door, her hands splayed with Grant's hands acting as shackles around her wrists. He tasted her mouth, her throat, sucking at her lips, her skin, sending rippling sensations down her spine. His breath was hot. Her body felt overheated.

When he released her hands, she left them splayed against the door and let him explore her body freely. It took every ounce of restraint not to curl her fingers through his hair. But it took more determination to remain standing on her unsteady legs.

He slid his hands along her arms, tickling the soft underside of her forearms, then framed her breasts. She ached for him to touch her, flesh to flesh. She tugged at his shirt in frustration.

Heavy-lidded with desire, his gaze traveled down her body, melting away her T-shirt with the heat of his gaze. His fingers drifted along her rib cage, tickled her sensitive skin, teased the hem of her shirt. Then his hands were on her skin, testing, sliding, touching. He cupped her breasts, rubbed a thumb across her nipples. She arched her back and groaned with pleasure...or pain. She wasn't sure which. She simply knew she wanted—needed—more. Now.

Finally she could stand no more of this torture. She yanked and pulled at his shirt. A button popped off and slid across the floor. The frenzy and the delicious hunger made her wild. A low moan in his throat prodded her.

Her shirt fell to the floor. His followed.

The heat made them reckless. Greedy. Wild.

Soon she stood naked, her body quivering, her skin burning. She felt his gaze glide along her skin, arousing, setting her on fire.

His build was finer than she'd imagined. The morning glimpse of his chest had stirred ideas, prompted fantasies. But here he was now, accessible.

They watched each other for a moment, gauging, speculating, taking deep gulps of air. His clothes lay intertwined with hers, a symbol of what was about to happen with their bodies. It made her restless, eager, insatiable.

She moved forward, but he stopped her with a hand to her shoulder. "Annie—"

"Please don't tell me you've changed your mind."

"No, but—"

"I know you don't want marriage. I don't, either. I just want this...you...now."

Both hands gripped her shoulders. "Annie, are you sure about this? Really sure? I mean, you and Griff never even..."

"I know that. But I'm not a virgin, Grant. I know what I'm doing."

"I just—"

She closed the gap between them, wrapped her arms around his shoulders and pulled his mouth to hers. "Shut up and kiss me."

He did.

She rubbed against him, letting her breasts tease his chest, and felt her skin tighten, her nipples harden. His chest hair was thick but soft. She ran her hands over the heat of his skin, and his muscles flexed beneath her fingers. She touched his erection, felt the throbbing heat along her palm, and a shudder ripped through him.

"Annie," he rasped.

"I want you," she said, her tongue toying with his.

When she dipped her head and sampled the salty sweat pearling on the skin of his chest, he groaned and said, "You've got me."

She bent low and, while cupping him gently, she slid her mouth around him, her tongue along his length. His hands braced against her shoulders as she drew him inside her mouth, then back.

Then he pulled her up to him, kissed her hard and gave her a there's-no-going-back look. He knelt before her, his hands slowly gliding down from her shoulders, over her breasts, teasing her flesh, making her knees liquid. He splayed his hand across her abdomen and down lower. With his fingers he teased her folds, rocked his hand back and forth against her in a slow then rapid motion.

Arching her neck, she pleaded, "Grant, please...!"

He nodded, turned away, dug for something in his pants pocket. She heard the crinkling of foil and a knowing smile born of relief tugged at her.

Then he came to her and lifted her slightly until he'd entered her. For a moment, they were still, their gazes locked. He filled her completely, made her restless for more. They began to rock together, the motion growing more urgent. She clung to him, wrapping her arms around his shoulders, burying her face in his neck.

Tiny shivers arced through her, growing with intensity and magnitude, overwhelming her. She bucked against him. A ragged sob tore from her throat. Grant gave a final thrust and called her name. Together, they slumped to the floor, limp, listless, replete. Their limbs were intertwined, their skin slick with sweat.

"Wanna go climb into the bed now?" she asked.

THIS WAS A FIRST. Usually he wanted to fall asleep after sex. But right now, with Annie snuggled against his side, her hand idly toying with his chest hair, he felt himself stir. Making love with her hadn't eased the wanting. It had somehow made it stronger, more powerful.

Now he knew what it felt like to be inside her. He knew the soft purr she made, her moan of pleasure, and he wanted to hear it again. This time he wanted it slow. He wanted to take his time. She'd caught him off guard before. She'd overwhelmed him. He should have at least brought her to the bed. But he couldn't have stopped himself from pushing her up against the front door any more than he could have stopped breathing. With a smile, he wondered if his neighbor across the hall had heard anything.

"What's so funny?" she asked, pushing up to her elbow.

He rubbed the smile off his face. "I'm surprised we haven't heard from old man Cummings."

"Who?"

"He lives across the hall. He's the hall monitor, or so we call him."

"Ah." She laughed. "I bet he thought you were trying to break out of your apartment."

"How's your back by the way?" he asked, concern nettling inside him.

"I'm fine."

She gave a slight shrug that lifted a breast. He reached out and cupped it, rolled the nipple between his fingers, and he immediately grew hard again. He shifted to his side and brushed her hair back from her face. Her skin was sticky with perspiration, her hair damp.

The corners of her eyes tilted upward and a gleam brightened the center. "What were we talking about?"

"Who cares?"

She laughed and touched her forehead to his. "Who would have figured this would have happened?"

"Me."

"You! When?"

He skimmed his fingers along her arm, entwined his with hers. Their palms flattened against each other. "You knocked me for a loop with that first kiss."

"Oh, yeah." She dipped her chin. "I'd forgotten about that. That's when we met, although I didn't know it at the time."

"Some hello."

She grinned, a dimple creasing one cheek. "Yeah." She pressed her body against him. She felt soft, warm, willing. "I never thought New York could be so much fun."

"Better than Lockett?"

"Oh my, yes."

"Things like this don't happen in Lockett?" he asked.

"Sure. But not in privacy. I mean, if you went to the lake with a boy and made out, it was all over town by midnight."

"So did you go to the lake often?"

"No."

"Oh, come on."

"I didn't. I wasn't very popular with the boys back home."

He couldn't believe that. "Why not?"

"I guess I was too different. Too demanding. Too dreamy. Too...much."

"Then I'm glad you came to New York." He skimmed his finger down her jawline. "I'm glad we met."

"Me, too." She looked away as if uncomfortable with the turn of the conversation.

Curious, he asked, "If you didn't like it back home, why'd you stay so long?"

She sighed. "I guess I didn't know my options. And...well, after my folks died—"

"When was that?"

"Mama died when I was sixteen. Papa when I was twenty-three, shortly after I graduated from Texas Tech."

He smoothed his hand along her cheek. "So young."

She didn't say anything for a moment. "I'd always dreamed of leaving home. But then...I don't know. I guess I wanted my family back. And I didn't think I'd find a home somewhere else.

"Do we have to talk about this now?" she asked, her hand sliding over his hip and cupping his buttock.

"Yes." He dipped his head and kissed her neck. "But don't worry, we'll shut up in a minute."

"Promises, promises."

"Is that why you kept wanting to get married?"

"Maybe. I wanted a family, a home, a place to call

my own. I own my folks' house, but it's filled with sad memories. Everything about it, from the porch swing to the electric stove, reminds me of them and...all I've lost. I wanted to escape those memories." She put her hand to his chest. "Don't get me wrong. I don't want to forget my parents, just not have their memories haunting me. And it wasn't just the house, it was everything. I remembered going for my first ice-cream cone with Papa to the soda shop. The grocery store reminded me of shopping with Mama...and her cooking—she was a fabulous cook. You know, she always said the way to a man's heart was through his stomach. But I think I've found a better way." She shimmied her hand down between their bodies and gripped him.

A groan pushed its way out of his throat. "Annie..."

She started nibbling on his ear then worked her way down his throat. He moaned and pulled her fully against him, felt the springy hair hiding her sex, the weight of her leg as it draped across his, her breath hot and urgent. A power he couldn't control took over his mind and body until he lost himself inside her.

# 11

SLICES OF LIGHT penetrated the room. Grant stirred and rolled to his side. He caught a whiff of something exotic, something elusive. Annie.

His eyelids snapped open. What had he done? Had he been drunk? No. Had he lost his mind? Possibly.

Without twitching a muscle, he glanced beside him. Rumpled bedsheets were the only reminder of what had taken place last night with Annie. That and his vivid memory of every touch, kiss and pleasure.

Shoving his fingers through his hair, he wondered where she was. Had she left? Hightailed it back to Texas? No way. She wasn't the type to run from anything.

Then he heard the shower spray in the bathroom. He debated about whether or not to join her. His body was definitely up for it. But doubts stopped him cold. What did she expect now? What did she want from him? A walk down the aisle? Surprisingly, that didn't sound as bad as it once might have.

Last night she'd talked about how she really didn't have a home, not one where she felt comfortable, safe, free. Well, he had that. But he had no one to share it with. Up until now, that had never bothered him. For some insane reason, it did at this moment.

He used to like the solitude the morning brought.

But now he yearned to wake up with Annie next to him, pull her close and kiss the sleepiness out of her eyes. He didn't want to face that today she would begin looking for her own place to live. He didn't want her to leave.

That thought scared his senses straight and kept him from joining her in the shower. He had to get his equilibrium back, figure out what he was going to say to her. Shoving back the covers, he pulled on a pair of jeans and paced the length of the room. When he noticed her clothes lying across the end of the bed waiting for her return, he decided he should take refuge in the kitchen. No need making things more awkward than they already were.

Before he could retreat though, she opened the bathroom door and a puff of steam rose around her. He smelled the delicate scent of a fragrant shampoo, something floral, and the clean odor of soap. She held a damp towel around her body; the material clung to her curves, made his body respond. Her blond hair fell in short, wet streaks around her face. Without even a bat of the eye, she smiled, kissed him on the mouth and dropped her towel to the floor.

Here was a woman who was uninhibited and sexy enough to drive him wild for years to come. *Whoa!* What was he thinking?

"Uh, Annie..." he said, squirming inside his skin. Wanting her, but not wanting her to get the wrong idea.

Was it too late for that? He braced his hands on her shoulders and forced himself to look at her eyes...not lower. "Look, uh..."

"Good morning." She moved closer and rubbed her body against him.

His reaction was immediate and intense. He held her close, enjoyed another kiss, this one deeper, hotter. His mind battled his body. What difference would one more kiss make? He wanted her. That was no secret. But...how much did he want her? What price was he willing to pay?

He settled his hands at her waist, but she broke the kiss first, leaving him feeling confused and slightly rebuffed.

She stared up at him, blinking slowly as if coming out of a trance. "What's wrong?"

"Nothing."

"Tired from last night?" Her voice dropped to a sensual tone.

"Uh, yeah." But he wasn't. He wanted her even more than he had then. He fisted his hands to keep from grabbing her, kissing her, taking her back to bed.

With an indifferent shrug that made her breasts sway enticingly, she turned away and presented him with a nice view of her sweet backside. He stared at the sunlight penetrating his room and tried to banish his thoughts, his need of her.

It didn't work.

"I know you're probably in a hurry to get to work." She picked up a brush out of her open suitcase and began to comb the strands of her hair.

He wanted to yell, "Cover yourself." But then he didn't want her to. He couldn't seem to get enough of the sight of her, much less the taste and feel of her. He took a step toward her, then thought better of it and veered toward the window. He listened to the street sounds from below—car horns blaring, the constant whir of traffic, somebody singing off-key. "Look, Annie..."

She stopped brushing her hair and turned to face him. "Oh, no. Here it comes."

"What?" Damn if he couldn't stop looking at her. And he didn't mean her eyes.

"The lecture. You know, where the man says he hopes I didn't get confused about what last night meant." She grinned. "It's okay, Grant. I understand. Just let me say it first."

"What are you talking about?" What was *he* talking about?

"Grant," she said calmly like a prim schoolteacher, except that her standing naked in his bedroom didn't conjure up any pictures of prudish schoolteachers that he knew. "I've always played by the rules. I always loved someone before I made love to them. Or at least what I thought love was at that time. But this is my new life."

He sank onto the edge of the bed, wondering if that meant she didn't love him. That was good, right? But it sure as hell didn't feel so good.

"I don't want to be promiscuous, but why should we resist what we both want? I mean, you do want me, don't you?"

Stunned by her words, he could only answer honestly. "Yes."

"And I want you—but not permanently." She smiled, the corner of her mouth pulling to one side, dimpling one cheek. It was a sympathetic, under-standing smile. He felt his stomach contract. "No offense."

"None taken." He'd told women at the beginning of all his relationships that he didn't want any strings attached, but he'd never had a woman want the same thing.

"I'm sorry," she said, moving toward him.

"For what?"

"Well, I'm not as sophisticated as the women you're used to. I probably handled this all wrong."

"I don't think there's a manual for how it's to be handled."

"None by Emily Post?" she joked.

"Not that I'm aware of."

He trailed his fingers along her collarbone, marveling at the silky texture of her skin, the warmth, the hint of soap and woman. She moved between his knees and settled her hands on his shoulders, then toyed with the hair at his nape.

He focused on the fact that she wanted him—as much as he wanted her. For today. Tomorrow didn't matter.

His hand slipped down to smooth a water drop over her nipple. Her skin puckered—an invitation he readily accepted.

"Don't you have to get to work?" she asked, her voice husky and warm.

"Don't worry. There's plenty of time for that."

BUT TIME BECAME her enemy late that evening. Annie took out her frustrations on the round steak, pummeling it with a wooden mallet. Grant had left her a message he wouldn't be home from work until late. But how late? And why? Was he avoiding her?

During the late afternoon, she'd helped the hours pass by getting to know the "hall monitor." Harvey Cummings had turned out to be a nice elderly man, a little paranoid, but definitely nice. He was a retired schoolteacher and had given her several names to call tomorrow.

Then she'd wandered downstairs and hung out in the lobby for a while, chatting with Bert the doorman. He was an out-of-work actor who was one play away from stardom.

She glanced at the clock on Grant's stove top—a quarter to eight. Her stomach rumbled. The water in the pan began to boil and she dumped in the cubed potatoes.

By the time she'd battered the steak and started it frying in the gourmet pan she'd found in one of Grant's cabinets, he arrived home. She heard the click of the door closing, then the squeak of the kitchen door opening.

"Hi," she said, feeling a bit shy but relieved. Her skin tightened with anticipation when she saw the bouquet of daisies in his hand. "Rough day at the office?"

Strain pulled at his features. "A demanding client, but nothing I can't handle."

"Well, then..." She moved toward him and hugged him close. "What you need is one of my famous massages."

"Sounds good."

"Are those for me?" she asked, looking at the daisies, smelling their sweetness.

"Yeah, sorry—I'm not good at being romantic."

"I don't want romance," she said, "but I do love flowers." She raised on tiptoe, wrapped her arms around him and offered him a kiss. "Thank you."

"You're welcome."

"Dinner will be ready soon." She stopped. "You didn't already eat, did you?"

"Nope. Didn't have time. Besides, I was hoping—"

"That I'd cook?"

He laughed. "No, that we might order a pizza and eat it in—"

"The bathtub?"

He shook his head.

"On the roof?"

He grinned.

"Oh, the bed! Well, we'll have to do that little fantasy tomorrow. As good as pizza sounds, I've already started chicken-fried steak."

"My favorite."

"Really?"

"Besides a good rib eye."

"You can take the boy out of Oklahoma but you can't take Oklahoma out of the man. Right?"

"Must be."

She started to turn back to the stove but he caught her around the waist and nuzzled her neck. Tiny sparks erupted along her spine. She arched into him, reveling in his strength, the security she felt in his embrace. His hand cupped her breast and ribbons of need curled through her.

"Smells good," he said.

She laughed, freeing some of the tension tightening her shoulders. "Me or the steak?"

"Hmm. Tough question." He grinned. "Ask me again after we eat."

A FEW MINUTES LATER, they sat at the kitchen table. Grant poured the thick creamy gravy she'd made over the chicken-fried steaks and mashed potatoes he'd piled on his plate. Annie had purposefully not lit candles or dressed up the table. It was better to keep things simple, uncomplicated.

"I'm surprised you didn't make hot dogs, corn dogs or French fries," he said. "Isn't that your usual fare?"

"You can't eat junk all the time. A girl's got to have nourishment."

"You're not like most women I know who pick and nibble things to death."

"Is that good or bad?"

"Definitely good."

"Why do they do that? Is it a New York tendency?" she asked, worrying she might not fit into this big-city life.

"Not that I know of. Tends to be a female thing."

"Not where I come from." She grinned. "We west Texas women like our food." She looked at his full plate. "Looks like boys from Oklahoma do, too."

"I haven't had a home-cooked meal since..." he paused and the corners of his mouth pinched "...since my mother was alive."

"How long has it been?" she asked.

"Five years in October."

"And you haven't had chicken-fried steak in that long?"

"Oh, sure, occasionally at the few restaurants that offer it here."

"I guess it is a southern delicacy," she said, wondering if she'd eventually start to miss Texas, Lockett or her friends. Aunt Maudie—she'd definitely miss seeing her aunt.

That thought reminded her that she needed to call her soon. But what would she say? "Funny thing happened when you went out to get me French fries on my wedding day. I ended up with the wrong groom."

Or was Grant the right one?

Unnerved by that thought, she said, "You don't cook much yourself, do you?"

"Not much. How did you know?"

"Everything was too clean. The utensils too shiny. But you had everything I needed." In more ways than one.

"I like to be prepared."

She remembered.

With a blush, she remembered his ease at reaching to get protection. She wondered how many women had sat in this very seat, sipping coffee or wine or bottled water. The sharp pang of jealousy surprised her, unsettled her.

She jumped up from the table to retrieve the salt and pepper shakers—contemporary shaped, they fit together like lovers spooning, then separated easily, like Grant and her would have to do. Sooner or later. She hoped it would be the latter.

"How was your day?" he asked, sounding too familiar, too much like a husband might. "What'd you do?"

She settled back into the wrought-iron chair that was surprisingly comfortable. Or maybe it was sitting across from Grant that felt so right. "What is it with New York? I mean, how does anybody afford a place to live here?"

"Roommates, good jobs."

She refrained from asking if he was offering to be her roommate. She wanted more—which made her insides tremble. Not again, she thought, and steeled her emotions against tumbling into love so easily.

"You must make a lot more money than teachers," she said.

"I do all right." He cut into his steak. "Where'd you look?"

"My feet feel like I walked all over Manhattan."

"How about a foot massage later?"

"And a hot bath."

Their eyes locked and it seemed as if everything they'd experienced together passed between them at that moment. The air sizzled.

She cleared her throat. "That's another problem. Nothing is available. How does anybody find a place to live?"

"Obituaries."

"You're kidding!"

"Partly." He covered her hand with his. A warmth flowed from him to her, filling her, calming her. "Don't worry. You can stay here as long as you need to."

"You might get sick of me pretty fast."

"I doubt it." The texture of his voice resonated inside her.

Was he serious? "And then there's the job market," she railed. "Maybe I could get a waitressing job until something opens up."

"Something will. Don't worry."

"Easy for you to say."

He paused and looked at her closely. "No, it's not. But I know you can find something."

"How do you know?"

"Because I know you. You can do anything."

Full of doubts, she snorted. He laced her fingers with his. She felt his strength, his gentleness. She wanted to curl up beside him, lay her head on his broad shoulder and forget her troubles...until tomorrow.

"If you can turn a disastrous wedding into a personal triumph," he said, "then I have no doubt you can find the job of your dreams and a decent apartment in this overcrowded city."

"Really?"

"Really."

"Well, I do have a few leads, thanks to Harvey."

"Harvey?"

"Old man Cummings. You know, your neighbor across the hall. He used to teach school and he gave me several names to call. I doubt anything will come of it but it's worth a shot. And then Bert had some leads for me, too."

"Bert?" he asked, a frown lining his forehead.

"Yeah, the doorman. Nice guy, Bert. Maybe we should double date sometime with him. He's got a girlfriend. They live together in Soho, wherever that is. They're both actors looking for work. Must be a tough life."

"What kind of leads did Bert give you?"

"Oh, apartment leads. I'll track them down tomorrow. He said his girlfriend might be able to get me a waitressing job where she works."

She sighed and pushed her empty plate toward the middle of the table. "There's nothing like comfort food to ease stress." She rubbed her temples. "I don't want to think about finding a job or apartment anymore tonight."

"Okay," he agreed. "Maybe I can help take your mind off your worries."

"I bet you can."

"Want to go out for ice cream? A movie?"

"Let's go to bed." Her invitation lay between them, bold and brassy.

"To sleep?" He eyed her as if unsure of what she expected after last night.

"Are you tired?" she asked.

"No."

"Good." She came around the table and sat on his lap, wrapping her arms around his neck. "Then let's go."

"Together?"

"Something wrong?" she asked, standing, resting her hand lightly, almost possessively on his shoulder.

"Uh, no. I just..."

"What?"

"I guess I'm just not used to a woman not wanting something more out of a relationship."

"Oh, I want something more," she said, hooking his arm around her waist.

"What's that?" His eyebrows raised as if he expected her to say something ludicrous like marriage.

"This." She placed her hands on either side of his face and kissed him, showing instead of telling him exactly what she wanted when they turned in for the night.

SHE WORE WHITE, of course. As she had planned to wear three times before.

Pale roses the color of blush, lilac and butter, the hues darker at the tips, lined the aisle. Lavish satin bows hung from the end of each pew. Virginal-white rose petals speckled the red carpet separating the groom's from the bride's side of the chapel, daring her to take a step toward her groom.

*Give me a break!*

Annie rolled to her side, pulled a pillow over her head and snuggled deeper into her dream, where her conscious mind couldn't mock her.

She glided, almost floated, toward the altar...toward Grant. He wore the typical tux, but there was nothing typical about him. His solemn look gave him an intensity. He wore power well and intimidated most men with a mere glance. Women tried to attach themselves to him like Velcro, but Annie was the only one who had stuck. He was hers. All hers.

Smiling at her groom, she was only dimly aware of the crowd of family and friends gathered. She fixed her gaze on Grant, believing if she blinked even once he might disappear like her other fiancés had. Before she could reach him. Before she could marry him.

Music filled the chapel with a swell of anticipation. When she reached Grant's side, she took a deep, jubilant breath. He was still here. She knew without a doubt that this was right.

She reached out for his hand, but he kept looking at her as if she'd grown an extra arm.

"What are you doing here?" he asked.

*What?* she wondered. *It's my dream. Don't I have a right to be here?*

"You said you didn't want a relationship." He gestured toward the candelabras, flowers and ribbons. "You didn't want this."

"I changed my mind," she said. Wasn't that a woman's prerogative? It certainly had been her previous fiancés'. "I want you, Grant. I love you."

"I haven't changed my mind. *This* isn't what I want."

*I don't want you* is all she heard. *I don't want you. I don't want you.*

Annie jerked to a sitting position. Blinking against the darkness that suddenly felt suffocating, she gulped several breaths. "It was a dream," she whispered to herself. "Only a dream."

Her mind raced as fast as her pulse. What had she been dreaming? And why? A wedding? Hers? And Grant...

*Oh my!* She inched away from the man who lay beside her in bed. Her heart pounded, a staccato beat, frantic and rapid like the sound of footsteps running. What had she done? What was she doing dreaming of their wedding? She didn't want to get married. She wanted her own life. She should never have given in to her impulses and gone to bed with Grant. What a fool she'd been—to think she could make love and not be in love.

Finding something else for her mind to worry over, she wondered what day it was. Was it even day yet? From the darkness, she guessed it was still night or too early in the morning to rise. But how long had she been asleep?

These thoughts of dates and time occupied her mind and kept memories and thoughts of Grant at bay, temporarily. She looked at the bedside clock. Unfortunately, it was located on Grant's side of the bed. His pillow blocked the red glowing numbers from her view.

She leaned closer without touching him, even though she longed to run her hand over his firm chest muscles, that wiry yet soft matting of hair. She felt his steady breathing, felt his warmth summoning her. Her mind translated the dark shadow sprawled across the bed into flesh and bone. She knew how every inch of him looked, how he felt, moved, tasted and loved. His nearness gave her an itch way down deep.

She resisted touching him though. She had to restrain herself. After all, she was *not* going to get serious with anyone, especially Grant. He didn't want a relationship or a commitment, and neither did she.

Then why had she dreamed it?

She didn't want to ponder that question. Tomorrow, as soon as the sunlight hit the horizon, she'd bound out of bed and search harder for a job and apartment. She had to get out of here. Before it was too late. Before she lost her heart.

She'd already grown too fond of Grant, too dependent on him, too obsessed with him. *Too fond? Too dependent? Ha! Maybe* obsessed *is a better word.*

*You said you love him.*

*It was a dream,* she countered, one side of her lining up against the other. And she wasn't exactly clear which side was which.

"What's wrong?" Grant asked, his deep, low voice startling her.

She jumped back to her side of the bed and pulled the sheet over her bare breasts. "I'm sorry. I didn't mean to wake you."

He pulled her toward him, his arms folding around her, warm, comforting, intoxicating. He settled her into the crook of his arm.

*Steel yourself! Don't think about your reactions, needs and desires!*

She knew better than to tell herself not to react to Grant. That was impossible. But could she stop needing him?

"Are you okay?"

*No.* "Yes." Her voice came out a tiny squeak. At least she would be all right when she forgot about Grant—*if* she could forget about him. But she had a feeling that might prove futile.

His hands started to roam over her. Already he knew where to touch her, how to stir and arouse. With feather-soft caresses, he teased the soft underside of her arm, the lily-white curve of her breast and meandered down to her center, her core. She sucked in a harsh breath and felt herself falling once again.

Having him make love to her was *not* the best way to forget about him, she realized. But at the moment her willpower waned. Procrastination, she decided, wasn't such a bad thing.

She'd forget him...tomorrow.

BY WEDNESDAY, Annie walked up and down more streets, made more phone calls and handed out her résumé to more schools. She also, in a desperate move, began applying for waitressing jobs, secretarial positions and even for the position of cashier in a local cinema. But without much experience carrying a tray of drinks or typing with any speed, she didn't hold out much hope for those possibilities.

That night, once again, Grant arrived home late. She already had a homemade chicken pot pie in the oven and salad tossed.

"Smells good," he said as he had every night that week.

"Me or dinner?" she asked, tilting her head as he nuzzled the length of her neck. Tiny eruptions burst along her spine in response, but a weight of exhaustion restrained her from looping her arms around his waist.

"You don't have to cook for me."

"I'm doing it for me, too."

"Always hungry, huh?" He chuckled, then straightened when she didn't respond. "What's wrong?"

"Nothing much." She sighed and turned away. She felt trapped and in desperate need of escape. But she knew the shackles were tied around her heart and bound her to Grant.

Maybe, she pondered, fear was making her want to stay with him. Was she afraid of her new life? Of beginning again? Or of failing?

While she stood at the stove, he wrapped his arms around her and pulled her back snug against his solid chest. "You don't seem yourself."

"Maybe this is a side of me you don't know."

"That's possible." He laid his cheek against the top of her head. She couldn't deny that he made her feel safe, loved and a whole lot of other physical things that she should put a lid on. "But I don't think so." He turned off the oven and pulled her into the living room. "Come here."

"Dinner is almost ready."

"It can wait."

"It might burn."

"Let it." He sat in an overstuffed chair and pulled her onto his lap. Together they faced the window overlooking The City. The glittering lights had once seemed luminous, full of promise and possibilities. Now they looked ominous and filled her with doubts and dread.

Afraid to meet his gaze, fearing he might see the confusion, the frustration and most of all her love for him in her eyes, she ducked her head, toyed with his tie. "You look nice."

"Thanks."

"Do you always dress so well for work?"

"Annie—"

"What is it that you do anyway?" she asked, trying to keep the conversation off her. "What exactly is an investment banker?"

He settled back, securing his arms around her. His thumb idly rubbed against her arm, drew patterns and raised goose bumps along her skin. "I put deals together," he said as if accepting she wasn't willing to discuss herself. "I find companies that have great potential and help them find backing so they can go public."

"Public?"

"On the stock market."

"Oh." She flipped the end of his tie upward then back down and smoothed her hand down the silk, feeling the bulges and slopes of his chest muscles. "Are you working on something now? A deal, that is?"

"Yes."

She lifted her gaze to meet his. He was intelligent, she knew that, but he was also successful. He wore it casually, not taking it or himself too seriously, not boasting about this deal or that, the way Griff always had. Or maybe Grant didn't think she'd understand! After all, she was a small-town girl...woman. Her stomach clenched.

"What are you working on now?" she asked.

"A couple of deals. One that's big. Really big."

"Are we talking millions?"

"Billions."

She choked. He said it so casually, as if he was talking about a nickel he'd found on the sidewalk. "I'm impressed."

"Don't be. It won't be all mine. I'm just the middleman."

"You put it all together."

"Yeah. But this one's proving more difficult than usual."

"How come?"

He hesitated. His finger tapped lightly on her shoulder as if he was weighing whether she could understand the intricacy of his work. "The owner of the company is...temperamental."

Annie began to knead his shoulders. "I'm sure you'll get it all worked out. And if not..."

"Then I could lose my shirt."

A wry grin pulled at her mouth. She tugged loose his tie. "Yeah, but I know how good you look without it. You'll be okay."

He covered her hand with his, stilling her movements to unbutton his shirt. With a voice as calm and patient as a father, he asked, "Are you ready now?"

The thought of her father brought a pang of despair to the center of her chest. She would have loved to have been able to call up her dad and ask for his advice.

She'd lost her parents too young. Usually she only felt alone on holidays, even though neighbors, friends and especially Aunt Maudie always included her in their own family celebrations. But today she felt lost, adrift, and very much alone, like a brown crusty leaf floating, twirling on the top of a slow-moving river, a victim of circumstance, at the mercy of the current's whim.

"I'm thinking maybe I should go home," she stated, detaching her voice from her constricting emotions.

"To Texas?"

She nodded. "To Lockett."

"Why?"

She couldn't tell him she needed to escape his influence, the way he made her feel, the way he made her hope, wish, long for something more between them. No, she'd told him she didn't want a relationship. She wouldn't change her mind. Too bad, her heart wasn't listening.

"I'm not qualified for a job here."

"Sure you are. There are lots of things you could do."

"But I want to teach. I could do that in Lockett."

"Give New York a chance. You've only been trying a few days. That's nothing."

"It's hopeless." She was hopeless. A hopeless romantic. A hopeless fool for falling once again for another man. A man who didn't want marriage. When would she learn? How many failed weddings would it take? Was she dense?

"Let me make a few calls," he offered.

"No. I have to do this on my own."

"I understand. I respect that, but—"

"I'll give it till Friday," she said. "Then I'm packing my bags and going home."

His arms tightened around her. She remained on his lap for a long time as they both stared out the window onto The City. Building lights twinkled like stars, reminding her of the far-reaching Texas sky. This place wasn't home. But why did she feel as if she belonged permanently in Grant's arms?

GRANT PACED his office all Thursday morning. He couldn't concentrate on the deal he was working out. Hell, he couldn't think of anything but Annie. Would she really leave if she didn't find a job by today?

He'd offer her a position working for him, but he'd known she wouldn't take it. She wanted to do this on her own. She had something to prove to herself. But what would returning home prove? Nothing.

He sipped his coffee that had turned cold hours before. He barely tasted the bitter liquid. Dammit, the problem wasn't finding Annie a job. Even if she found one, she still wanted her own place, her independence. He couldn't blame her, especially after all she'd been through with Griffin and her other fiancés. But the thought of her moving out brought a sharp pang to his chest.

The real problem was Annie. He didn't want her to leave New York, much less his apartment. But how could he stop her?

Once again, for the fifth time that day, he grabbed the phone and dialed his home number. Every time he'd called before, the answering machine had picked up. He hoped Annie was pounding the pavement in search of a job. This time, though, she answered on the second ring.

"Annie?"

"Yeah?

"Uh..." He hadn't thought about why he was calling, what he was going to say. Frankly, he'd just wanted to hear her voice, just wanted to assure himself that she hadn't left early. "How are you doing?"

"Fine."

"Did you go out this morning?"

"Yes."

He pushed a drawer of his desk closed with his thigh. She was being deliberately vague. He wasn't sure how hard he could press her. "Any word from...anybody?"

There was a long pause before she answered. "Who do you mean? Griffin?"

"My brother? No, I didn't mean..." His shoulders bunched. "Did he call?"

"No."

"Oh, well...good." He ignored the spike of jealousy in his heart, or tried to. "What about any of those places where you left your résumé yesterday?"

"I had an interview this morning."

"You did?" Hope surged within him, then fell flat. Why hadn't she told him about it? "How'd it go?"

"Well, it was one that Harvey helped set up. It sounds really wonderful, but I doubt I'm qualified."

"Why do you say that?"

"I just got a sense that, well...that they were looking down their nose at me. Probably my accent had something to do with it."

Grant jiggled the change in his pocket restlessly. "There's got to be a teaching job out there for you. After all, this city has a shortage of teachers."

"I have another interview this afternoon," she said, but there wasn't a trace of enthusiasm in her voice.

"That's terrific." He tried to sound optimistic.

Then he noticed his secretary staring at him from the doorway. He covered the mouthpiece with his palm. "What is it, Delaney?"

"Your two o'clock is here. And she's not happy about waiting."

He gave a slow nod. Susan never had been the patient sort. "Look, Annie, I've got to run. Good luck this afternoon. Call me when you get back, okay?"

"Why?" she asked. "There won't be anything to report, unless you want to know what time my plane leaves Saturday."

"Saturday!" Panic squeezed his gut. "Annie—"

"All flights were booked on Friday night." She sighed. "See you tonight."

He held the phone a long minute after the line went dead, then realized he was gripping it as if it were a lifeline. He slammed the phone into its cradle. "Okay, Delaney, send Susan in."

A moment later, Susan Wilkerson walked into his office with all the confidence of a corporate president. The tall, slender brunette, who had more angles than curves, strode right for him. He'd learned quickly that she was often more smoke than substance, especially when it came to her private life. Work on her dot-com company consumed her twenty-four hours a day, seven days a week. It made for a great client, but a not-so-great girlfriend.

Today, though, her usual professional demeanor had slipped. She grinned. "Did you see the *Times?*"

"Did the article make it in the business section?"

"Front page. Best piece of advertising we could get." She plopped her Coach briefcase, the expensive one he'd bought her six months ago, beside the leather chair opposite his desk. But she didn't sit down. She came around the desk, leaned her hip against the polished wood, shoving his papers out of the way and inching her skirt up her thigh. "Once we're up and running, our stock will soar. We'll be richer than you or I could have ever dreamed."

*We*, he thought, his nerves prickling with concern.

"How can I show my appreciation?" she asked. "Wanna celebrate?"

"Susan," he started, "we need to discuss our appointment next week with the California—"

"Let's talk about us." Her hands eased over his shoulders.

"Us? What us?" He clasped his hands around her toothpick arms and set her away from him. "We agreed that we weren't an item. That business and pleasure don't mix."

Giving him a petulant pout that didn't quite work

for her, she said, "But I miss the pleasure. I've missed you."

He tapped the folder on his desk. "We also need to discuss the press releases—"

"How was Texas? It felt like you were gone forever."

"Just a weekend."

"A long, lonely weekend."

"Look, Susan—"

She covered his mouth with her fingertips. "Did you meet someone?"

"What do you mean? I went away for my brother's wedding."

"Oh, yes, I forgot. Did he actually do it this time?"

"No, he bailed at the last minute."

She chuckled and leaned forward, angling her mouth to his, her breath bathing his lips.

"Susan," he said, stopping her advance, "we need to stick to our decision to keep this just business between us."

She sighed and shrugged a shoulder. Studying her nails, she said, "Does that mean you're not coming to my cocktail party Friday night?"

"No, I'll be there." But he wouldn't like it. He didn't want to lose her as a client, but he didn't want her as a girlfriend.

He wanted Annie. Only Annie.

STILL IN HER PAJAMAS at ten o'clock Friday morning, Annie padded around Grant's apartment. She should have been packing. Instead, she touched a silver frame on the corner of his desk, a horseshoe, a leather book.

This was her last day in New York. Her last day with Grant.

She couldn't shake the gloom that had settled over her. Her cold breakfast of eggs, bacon and toast remained on the kitchen table waiting for her appetite to arrive.

At five after ten, the phone rang, jarring her, frazzling her nerves. Her heart pounding, she hoped it would be Grant, that he'd say he was coming home to spend the rest of the day with her. But the voice on the other end wasn't Grant's. Still, it made her heartbeat scamper.

Jotting down the information with a shaky hand, she only managed to say, "Yes. Okay. Sure. Right."

As soon as she hung up the phone, she located Grant's office number. She had to place the call twice, as she entered it wrong the first time. "He's in a meeting," his secretary said, using a professionally detached voice.

"Oh, well...okay." Disappointment rippled through her.

"Can I take a message?"

"Tell him Annie called."

"Annie Baxter?"

Her pulse thumped in her temple. "Yes."

"One moment, please."

There was a humming silence on the line before she heard Grant's familiar voice. "What's up?"

"I got it!" She could no longer suppress the excitement coursing through her.

"A job?"

"Yes, of course, a job!"

"Where?"

"It's a teaching position at a private school. They're going to help me get my accreditation."

"Congratulations!"

"Thank you, Grant. I mean it—thank you."

"I didn't do anything. You got the job all on your own."

"Thank you for encouraging me, for helping me believe it could happen. Maybe I really am supposed to live here in New York."

"Of course you are. This is definitely something to celebrate. How about it?"

"Yes." She couldn't think of anyone she'd rather celebrate with. But her real celebration would be held in secret, in the corner of her heart—a celebration, not for the job, but for staying in New York...staying with Grant. At least for now.

# 13

*(the of battered tops of both potted plants, the salt flow one left propped against the door, if left to Lockett her. He figured that his wild, to see they'd already drawn in both, well-loved—be wanted to do just ...*

*believe. He once nearly replaced ... she'd said, "*

*Goddamn it. Enough was enough, he wanted to celebrate, to ...*

ANNIE MET GRANT at the door to his apartment with a smile and a kiss. He automatically dropped his briefcase and bracketed her waist, pulling her against him, deepening the kiss, the pleasure. He held her close, relieved and thrilled she wouldn't be moving back to Lockett, Texas, anytime soon.

Now he just had to figure out a way to keep her in his apartment.

"Thank you," she whispered against his mouth.

"For what?"

"For everything."

"Annie, I didn't do anything. You did it all. You made it happen."

"You helped me believe in myself, my abilities, that there was a job out there."

"It was easy," he said into the softness of her hair, "to believe in you."

Her embrace tightened, then she sniffed delicately and moved away. "So—" she gave a slow twirl, her arms outstretched "—what do you think? I bought it this afternoon for our celebration."

He gave her an appreciative gaze. She wore a slinky black dress that followed the gentle curves of her body that he knew so intimately. The simply constructed front contrasted with the alluring and arousing back that plunged to the sweet, low place at the base of her spine. It reminded him of how sensuously she moved, how she felt pressed against him, how it felt to be inside her. He remembered the wild things they'd already done in bed, and things he wanted to do later tonight.

*Tonight.* His brain slowly registered all she'd said. Celebration? Tonight? She wanted to celebrate tonight. He hadn't meant tonight. He couldn't take her out tonight. He had Susan's cocktail party to attend.

"Grant?" She tilted her head, staring at him as if baffled by his silence.

Damn. He'd have to figure something out. He'd much prefer to spend his evening with Annie rather than clients, especially Susan. Maybe they could delay the celebration until tomorrow.

"Grant?"

He shook loose his confusing thoughts and focused on her. "You're beautiful."

"I was talking about the dress. For a minute it seemed as if you didn't like it."

"No way." He hooked his hands at the small of her back, felt the intoxicating warmth of her skin. "You make it beautiful."

She snuggled up against him, wrapping her arms around his neck. Her fingers traced the line of his shoulder. "I'm hungry. Are you?"

"Definitely." He lowered his mouth to hers, tasted her deeply, thoroughly.

"I meant for dinner. I'll fix something—"

"Fix me." He sealed his mouth to hers, drew in her breath, until they became one.

With a quick, intricate move, he slipped the straps of her dress off her shoulders and the material pooled at her feet, leaving her nearly naked in his arms, except for delicate lace black panties.

"Grant!" Her eyes widened with shock at his unexpected move.

He grinned and cupped one of her bare breasts in the palm of his hand. "I told you, I'm hungry." He nuzzled her neck. "For you."

She tilted her head and allowed him more access. Her fingers began a march down his chest, unbuttoning his shirt and removing his tie, then unfastening his belt. "Well, then I'll just have to wait for dinner."

"Too much of a hardship?" he asked, sucking in a breath when she folded her hand along his length.

"Not hardly."

This time, she kissed him. Her hand moved in a slow rhythm that nearly drove him crazy with wanting. His hands roamed freely over her shapely backside, cupping her, kneading her taut muscles, pulling her closer to him. She lifted one knee and wrapped her leg around his hip. He slid his hand along her thigh until he reached the center of her and brought her to full arousal.

She groaned in his ear. "Oh, Grant, please, now."

"No," he said, his voice ragged and sharp. "Not here. Not this time."

Lifting her against him, he carried her away from the front door and into the bedroom. "Don't want you bruising your back."

"Guess it wouldn't look very good in that dress." She settled her other leg around his waist, her arms draped over his shoulders. "So, where are you taking me?"

"To bed."

She laughed. "Oh, how conventional!"

He shook his head and gently deposited her on the mattress. "You've been in New York too long. Whatever happened to the small-town girl I met in Lockett?"

"I've grown up." She pulled him down to her. "Did you ever really think of me as a girl?"

"Not after that first kiss."

He aligned his body with hers. His legs were longer, tanner, hairier than hers. Hers were smooth, silky and long enough to wrap around his waist. His hands sought hers, their fingers lacing. His mouth sampled all she had to offer.

He settled between her thighs and moved his body in rhythm with hers. His arms tightened around her. Then she cried his name, the breathy sound reverberating in his heart.

His heart pounding, he rolled to his side, pulling her with him, keeping them joined. Her hand lay against his chest. She gave him a lazy smile, her eyes glazed with wonder.

"How do you do that?" she asked.

"What?"

"You know…" A deep red blush stained her cheeks.

"Instinct." He pulled her into the crook of his arm. "It's mutual, you know."

"I know." Her finger tapped lightly against his heart as if knocking to get inside. But he knew she was already there, and it worried him.

Never had Grant felt so relaxed with a woman, so complete, so fulfilled. Annie could clear his head and fog his brain at the same time. She could pull a smile out of him or make him feel strong and protective. She amazed him.

This was no longer a casual relationship. Maybe it never had been. What they had certainly couldn't be tossed aside easily. Somehow he'd have to find a way for them to be together.

The answer seemed simple, yet too complicated.

"So," she said, sliding her fingers through his tousled hair, "where are we going for dinner?"

"Dinner?"

"Yeah. Remember? I said I was hungry. That's how we ended up here."

"Oh, I thought you took off your dress and that's when...you know."

"I didn't take off my dress! You did."

"I did?"

She laughed and tweaked one of his chest hairs.

"Ouch!"

Quickly, she covered the sensitive spot with her lips. "Wanna take me to dinner?"

"Definitely." But what about the cocktail party? Heck, he'd take Annie. He didn't owe Susan any explanations. "We could go dancing afterward."

"Sounds ro...wonderful."

Had she been about to say "romantic"? That was his intention but it also made him as nervous as a tourist crossing Forty-second Street.

He decided he should explain things to her, even though he planned to whisk into the party and then out without bumping into Susan. "Annie, would you mind if we stopped at a cocktail party first? It's for work."

"Is it about that deal you were telling me about?"

"Yes. This client isn't the easiest to work with."
He'd explain the situation to her. She'd understand.

"Not a problem. I can wait a little while before having you all to myself." She rubbed her breasts against his chest, jumbled his thoughts. "It won't cause a problem if I go, will it?"

"Not at all," he said, "but—"

"Let's hurry then. The sooner we go, the sooner we can get back here."

Not a bad plan, he decided.

SHE WASN'T in Lockett anymore. Annie stared out the cab window at the Waldorf Astoria's ornate entrance. The art deco hotel took up an entire city block on Park Avenue. She'd never seen anything like it. The Motel 6 back in Lockett didn't have the same ambience...or clientele.

"What do you think?" Grant asked, his breath hot against her nape.

"It's amazing."

He drew a finger down her spine, giving her a tingle in the pit of her stomach, then opened the cab door.

He alighted first, then held out his hand for her. His palm was warm and welcoming as he pulled her from the cab. She stood in the street and gawked like a tourist.

"Annie, before we go in you should know—"

"Look at that!" She raced forward, feeling like a little kid in a candy store.

"Annie!"

"I should have brought my camera."

"You're not a tourist anymore. You're a New Yorker."

"I don't feel like one yet."

"You will."

"I don't know if I'll ever get used to all this." Her head swam with all the sites she still wanted to see—Rockefeller Center, Radio City Music Hall, Ellis Island. She imagined waking on lazy Saturday mornings in Grant's arms, then setting out with him to see the sites.

She wasn't sure if the jittery sensations in her stomach were from the idea that New York was where she'd committed to live for the next year or from Grant's nearness and her uncertainty about her feelings for him.

He had changed into a tux after their lovemaking and a quick shower, probably the same one he'd worn for their "wedding." His good looks, steady hand at the small of her back and calm demeanor made her as giddy as a bride. But she wasn't his bride.

She could hope.

That was a huge leap in a new direction. She recognized the truth of it and knew she'd been deceiving herself over the past week. She couldn't forget Grant, couldn't treat their time together, their relationship, as casually as she would a pair of pants that she'd tried and discarded without another thought.

No, this was serious.

But why hadn't she realized it earlier? Maybe she had. Maybe that's why she'd wanted to run away. Maybe her new job had given her confidence, made her bold, allowed her to believe in far-reaching possibilities. Or maybe Grant had.

He touched her elbow, tried to restrain her. "Annie, I need to tell you—"

"It's okay, Grant—I won't embarrass you. I promise to act sophisticated, not in the least impressed by anything or anyone around me. I'll be a real New Yorker."

"That's not—"

The doorman gave them a polite nod and tipped the brim of his hat. The setting sun's warm hues of crimson and amber struck the glass door as he pulled it open. "Good evening."

"Hello." Annie stepped inside and marveled at the plush carpeting and grand staircase accented with brass rails. She felt like Dorothy about to enter the Emerald City as she started the climb.

"Annie," Grant said, his tone different than she'd ever heard from him. He sounded irritable. When they reached the top of the staircase, he led her to one side of the lobby and stopped.

"Something wrong?" She brushed the back of her hem to straighten it. "Am I flashing?"

His gaze flicked along the back of her. "No. You're fine. It's—"

"Don't worry," she said. "I'll watch my p's and q's."

"Annie, I... Ah, hell." Grant shoved his hands in his pants pockets. He seemed deep in thought, troubled.

"What's the matter?" she asked. "Have I done something wrong?"

He shook his head. "I have. Look, Annie, you need to know... What I've been trying to tell you is—" His gaze narrowed on something or someone across the lobby. "Damn. It's Susan."

The name stopped her cold. She felt a punch to her heart and it shattered on impact.

Susan? What did she have to know? Who was Susan?

His choice of words stunned her. She felt the sting as if it were a verbal slap. But the hurt went much deeper. She wasn't sure what he was about to say but she knew she wouldn't like it, knew it would shatter her make-believe world and possibly her heart.

Why was he doing this now? Here? "What do you mean, Grant? What are you saying? Who is Susan?"

He seemed suddenly distant, remote as her dreams had always been. Her nerves unraveled like a ball of Aunt Maudie's knitting. She felt vulnerable, exposed. The sound of laughter across the lobby magnified in her ears. Her stomach cramped.

"Damn, this is..." he paused for the right word "...awkward."

"Awkward?" she repeated dully. She felt numb for a brief instant then something flared inside her, ignited like a brushfire. "What's going on, Grant? Are you dating this Susan? Is she your client's daughter? His wife? What?"

"Annie, Susan is—"

"Grant!" From across the lobby a woman waved and approached them.

Annie watched the brunette who resembled Cindy Crawford. She was as slender as any model, as tall as the Statue of Liberty in her slinky high-heeled sandals. Her red dress put warning bells in Annie's head. The woman wore confidence like a tiara.

Annie looked toward Grant. His mouth had pulled into a straight line. She felt a sinking in her abdomen, a dizziness seize her, the lobby began to move slowly around her like a carousel.

"I'm so glad you were able to come," Susan said, sidling up to Grant and giving him a kiss right on the mouth. It was brief, but possessive, intimate.

The audacity!

The absurdity of this whole situation.

Never in all the times that she'd been dumped by her fiancés had she ever felt this humiliated, this devastated.

Annie folded her hands into fists. She felt a fire swell inside her. Grant was her man! Not Susan's.

Then a chill swept through her. It was the cold distance Grant had placed between them a few moments before. No, he wasn't hers. He wasn't hers at all. And it was her own damn fault.

She'd said she didn't want a relationship...romance. And look what had happened. How could she have fallen for a man like Grant? A man who wasn't even available.

"Susan," Grant said, settling his arm around Annie, "this is Annie Baxter. Annie, this is Susan Wilkerson."

Annie gave her a brief nod and felt the woman's distinct disapproval.

"Susan's the owner and president of we-sell.com. Her site makes ebay.com look like a dusty old flea market."

"Really?" Annie said tightly, not knowing what he was talking about. She wasn't very computer literate. To her, e-mail seemed impersonal. But why were they acting so civilized when all Annie wanted to do was punch Grant then Susan in the nose.

Maybe this was how they handled dalliances in New York. Maybe that's all she'd been to Grant. Had she ever asked if he was involved with someone? She couldn't remember. She couldn't think.

"She's one of my clients," Grant finished saying.

"I see."

"Well," Susan said, linking her arm with Grant's, "let's not trivialize our relationship, Grant. We've known each other awhile."

"Yes, Grant," Annie interrupted, "let's not trivialize the situation." She felt as if she was drowning. "Aren't you going to explain who I am to Susan?"

He nodded. "Of course. Susan, you remember I was in Texas last week."

"Ah, yes, for your brother's wedding." She placed her hand possessively against Grant's chest and turned her hazel eyes onto Annie. Her gaze seemed to contain slivers of ice. "You must be from Texas. I thought I recognized your quaint accent."

"Yes," she answered. "I'm from Texas."

"Have you known Grant long?"

"In some ways," she said, "in some ways not." In some ways she didn't know him at all.

Susan flicked a cutting glance over them. "Your name sounds familiar. You wouldn't happen to be Griffin's fiancée, would you?" She touched Grant's arm. "I remember you telling me that your brother was getting married to someone named Annie. I remember thinking what a sweet, childlike name that was. Wasn't the wedding last weekend?"

"No, it wasn't," Annie said, her voice fading.

"Look, Susan, we can't stay long. We wanted to drop by and—"

"Grant," Annie interrupted, "I don't intend to stay

at all. If you'll excuse me..." She turned and headed toward the door.

"Nice to meet you," Susan called after her, a cackle of triumph in her voice.

"Annie!"

She heard Grant's voice but she kept walking. She rushed past a group of tourists and made the revolving door practically spin on its axis. She pushed into the waning sunlight and blinked to gain her bearings. Everything was too loud, too bright, too much.

Grant caught her arm and turned her to face him. "Annie, it's not—"

"Please, Grant." She held up a trembling hand. She couldn't listen to any more. Poor excuses. Heartbreaking facts. "Stop."

Everyone in her hometown was right. She had the worst luck in love. Annie realized then that Grant was what she'd wished Griffin and her other two fiancés had been. He was her ideal man. And now he was history.

She choked on the words clogging her throat. "I loved you."

Her own shock was reflected in Grant's eyes. She felt the blood rush out of her head. Frightened, sickened by all of it, she turned and strode away, her pace clipped, the pieces of her heart rattling around inside her like broken glass.

She had no direction, no purpose, except escape.

She didn't care who this Susan was. It was all too obvious. She certainly didn't want the gory details. She no longer cared about anything, especially not about Grant.

"Annie!"

She heard her name lift above the din of traffic sounds. Ducking her head, she made a sharp right turn. A man in a dark suit muttered a curse as she stepped in his way. She jerked to a stop then stepped off the curb. Waving her arm, she shouted for a cab and miraculously one stopped almost at her feet. She yanked open the door and slipped inside.

"Where to?" the driver asked, staring at her in the rearview mirror. He had kind eyes, she thought, huge and dark.

She slammed the cab door closed. "Anywhere." She'd figure out the particulars later. "Just go."

He gave a brief nod and threw the car in gear.

WHEN GRANT SAW the cab Annie had escaped into pull away and mingle with traffic, a sea of yellow taxis surging and swelling around it, he stopped running. His breath came hard and fast but he knew it had nothing to do with the exertion of the chase.

Her confession rang in his ears, resonated in his chest. *I loved you.*

Past tense, he realized now. It left a residue of guilt and despair inside him. He didn't want her love. He didn't trust in it. After all, just last week, which seemed more like months than days, she'd been about to walk down the aisle to marry his brother. Love didn't die that fast. It didn't happen that fast, either. Maybe she'd simply transferred her affections for Griffin to him.

Even if love could, by some miracle, happen that fast, then it couldn't last. Her love would fade in time. But would his?

He clamped down on the truth beating within his

heart, suppressed it, crushed it like a tin can. He didn't want to love anyone, especially not Annie. She was the kind of woman who wanted fairy-tale endings. And she deserved them.

He retraced his steps to the hotel. Business would get his mind off Annie. But he wondered if it could stop the jagged edge of pain biting into his heart.

"I AM NOT RUNNING AWAY," Annie declared more to herself than the waiting cabdriver. She tossed her suitcase into the back seat and joined it.

The taxi driver, who she'd learned was named Raphael, gave her a long look. "Not my business."

"Well, I'm not!" She glanced one last time at Grant's apartment building and wondered if his landlady was taking notes from some inconspicuous window she used as a lookout.

Emotions, raw and fierce, attacked her heart as Raphael steered them toward the airport. Never had she felt this despondent, this heartbroken, not after Rodney dumped her, not after Travis ran out on her and not even when Griffin vanished the morning of their wedding. And it was all Grant's fault.

No. The blame lay with her. After all, she'd forced herself on him. But worse, she'd finally, truly been in love. The forever-and-ever kind her parents had shared.

But Grant didn't love her. She wasn't his type. Some Susan, who fit into the New York scene, who could wine and dine with the best of them, did. Annie was unsophisticated, inexperienced, a small-town hick. And definitely a loser when it came to love.

She clamped her hands together in her lap. "I am not running away."

She'd return to Lockett—temporarily. Long enough to pack her things and move them to New York. She might not get her man, but this crushing blow wouldn't stop her from living her life. Lifting her chin, she tried to keep the tears from falling recklessly down her cheeks.

But the thought of her wedding dress still hanging in Grant's closet, along with her hopes and dreams, unraveled her like a loose thread.

# 14

GRANT DOWNED three scotches without soda. He glared at the assortment of executives gathered at the Waldorf Astoria. The women wore glitzy jewelry, fancy clothes and had their hair done at the most expensive salons in New York. But none of them could come close to Annie's beauty, her brains, her spunk.

"Are you finished pouting?" Susan asked, settling her shoulder neatly against his.

"Nice crowd," he said.

"I invite only the best, the brightest, the most enjoyable." She gave him a heavy-lidded gaze. "So what's wrong with you?"

"Is that what I'm doing? Pouting?"

"I'd say so. And a pretty fair job of it, too."

"I always want to be the best at whatever I do."

Her hand slid down his arm. "You are. Believe me, you are."

"Susan—"

"I know. You're not interested in combining work and pleasure. That's too bad. Because work and pleasure are the same for me."

"I know that." He loved his job, too. But he'd realized over the past week that there was more to life.

"Did you meet Ethan?" she asked.

"Ethan?"

She nodded toward a jovial blond across the room downing drinks as fast as he was making deals.

"Stockbroker?" Grant asked.

"How'd you know?"

"Looks the type."

"Are you jealous?" she asked.

"Are you?"

"Of your little Texas filly?" She laughed. "Oh, please."

"I thought you wanted...I'm confused here, Susan. You're sending me mixed signals."

"No, I'm not. I'm the same. Remember? I'm the one who agreed that no strings was great. But you've changed."

"No, I haven't."

"You're a great investment banker, Grant, but a horrible poker player—at least when it comes to the game of hearts." She patted his arm and took his empty glass from him. "I'm sure you'll make a terrific husband, though."

His spine stiffened. "I'm not looking to get married."

"Yeah, but she is."

"Annie doesn't want marriage, either. She told me. She said no romance, no relationship, no—"

Susan tipped her head back and laughed. "Well, believe me, she's the marrying type." She dipped her finger into his glass and plopped a scotch-coated ice cube into her mouth. "And so are you, my friend. So are you."

ANNIE WAS GONE. Gone, gone, gone. Poof, she'd simply disappeared, stripping his apartment bare of all she'd brought with her. Without her scent, her presence, her smile, it felt empty. Grant lay down in the center of the bed and listened to the hum of silence surrounding, penetrating him.

He'd made his dutiful appearance at Susan's cocktail party then slipped away unnoticed. Susan's words chased each other around his brain. Denial ran a fast second.

Rushing home, he'd hoped Annie would be here waiting. He would have much rather had her throw a vase at him or punch him in the nose than to have had her vanish into the night. He deserved some kind of punishment, but did he deserve to lose Annie completely?

He caught sight of white silk shimmering through the barely opened door of the closet. It was like a flag of surrender. Her wedding dress. And it made him want...

Damn.

Jerking to his feet, he left the apartment, unable to tolerate the emptiness, the reminders. Even the ride down the elevator seemed lonely. What had happened to him? He loved his bachelorhood. He loved living alone. He loved being single.

He loved Annie.

*No. Don't even think it.*

"Evening, Mr. Stevens. Going out again?" Bert said.

Grant gave an automatic nod without really looking up or paying attention. Then a thought stopped him. Maybe the doorman knew where she'd gone.

*Not that I'm going after her.*

But he'd feel better if he knew she was safe. That's all.

"Did you happen to see Annie—Mrs. Stevens— leave this evening?" Since the whole building believed they'd been married in Texas, he had to continue the charade—even now when it hurt like hell.

Bert gave him a quizzical look.

"We were supposed to meet here and I think we missed each other," he explained, not wanting to say she'd left him for good.

"I don't think she was planning on meeting you, Mr. Stevens. I'm sorry."

Grant seethed inwardly. So everyone knew she'd left him, huh?

He crammed his hands in his pants pockets and took a step toward Bert. "Look, I just want to know she's okay."

"Oh?" Bert gave him a scornful look. "You didn't worry about her much while you were at your fancy cocktail party, did you?"

What was this? Lockett? Or New York City? Grant felt like he'd entered the Twilight Zone. Had Annie won everyone to her side? Was he the villain now?

He shoved his hand through his hair. "Is she all right?"

"Yes." Bert started to turn away but Grant grabbed him by the arm.

"Tell me where she went."

"Are you going after her?"

"No."

"Then what does it matter?"

"I just want to know."

Silence swelled between the two men, punctuated by the blare of a car horn. Grant tightened his grip on the doorman's lapel.

"She headed toward the airport."

Instantly, Grant released Bert. He knew she was going home to Texas, where she belonged.

Grant brushed the crinkles out of the doorman's jacket where he'd grabbed him. "Thanks."

Hunching his shoulders against the throbbing pain in his chest, Grant turned and walked away.

"Her flight was scheduled to leave at nine-twenty," the doorman called after him.

Grant didn't even bother to look at his watch.

With the darkness of night wrapping around him, the noise of the city blocking out his own thoughts, he walked aimlessly through his neighborhood. Up one street and down another, he kept to himself and continued walking, taking one step at a time.

He thought of his childhood in Oklahoma. His hometown had been much like Lockett, but his family had been much different from Annie's. He remembered his father's voice raised in anger. He could still hear the slam of a door as his mother retreated to her bedroom. The threats. The fear. The uncertainty.

He'd left there vowing never to marry, never to live that way. And he'd kept his promise. All he'd ever wanted was peace and he'd found it in the hustle and bustle of New York City. Strange, but it was true.

A giggle brought him out of his self-imposed trance. He noticed a couple strolling ahead of him, holding hands, kissing in the shadows of each awning. They laughed and smiled as if they shared a secret.

And he thought of Annie.

Never had he felt so alone, so lost, so at war with himself. Suddenly his peaceful existence was shattered.

When the streets no longer shielded him from his own pain, he returned to his apartment like a homing pigeon. Loneliness twisted around him like strangling vines. His apartment had always been a haven, a place to escape the busy, competitive business world. Now each corner, each place he looked—the kitchen stove, the couch and the bed—reminded him of Annie.

The blinking red light on the answering machine caught his attention. Hope shot through him and he raced toward it.

"Annie," he prayed as he punched the button to play the message.

"Hey, Grant! Annie!" His brother's voice reverberated through the apartment, sounding too loud, too boisterous compared to Grant's mood. "Thought I'd call before I headed back to Texas. I'm taking the red-eye tonight. Last chance if you want to go back with me, Annie."

Grant's hands folded into fists. Had Annie returned with Griffin? If so, he'd—

Griffin's laughter rang through the apartment. "I know, I know. You don't have to turn me down again."

A margin of relief sifted through Grant. Maybe Annie had bought her own ticket. Maybe she hadn't heard this message at all.

"Well, guess this is goodbye," Griffin said. "If you get this message before ten, you can catch me at the hotel." He gave his room number and hung up.

Grant stared at the phone for a long moment, then he glanced at the clock on the mantel. Annie's plane had probably already departed.

Stricken, he didn't know why he made the call or why he agreed to meet Griffin for drinks. But it kept him out of his apartment and, once more, he hoped it would keep Annie off his mind.

THE BAR WAS DARK, but not dark enough to match Grant's mood. He realized why he'd wanted to see his brother: he was a visible testament that someone could survive a relationship with Annie.

"How's Annie?" Griffin asked, lifting his Manhattan to his mouth and taking a sip.

Grant downed a scotch and ordered another. "I don't know."

His brother frowned. "What do you mean? I thought you said you'd watch over her. Take care of her."

"I didn't agree to marry her," he snapped.

Griffin gave him a hard stare. "I never said anything about marriage. I just wanted you to keep an eye on her, help her get her feet under her. Hell, she's from a small town. New York is as foreign to her as—"

"Annie can take care of herself. She's more capable than you give her credit for."

Griffin stared at Grant. "Something happened between you two, didn't it?"

Grant refused to answer on the grounds that he might incriminate himself. Instead, he reached for his second scotch.

His brother clamped his hand around Grant's arm.

Scotch sloshed over the edge of the glass. "Did you make a pass at her?"

"No." He certainly hadn't made the first move.

"Then what happened?"

"I fell in love." The words exploded in his head. But he wouldn't take them back; he couldn't deny the truth any longer.

He loved Annie. Now she hated him.

The sounds of glasses clinking, music blaring, people laughing and carrying on punctuated the stunned silence lying between the two brothers. Then Griff reared back his head and began to laugh. The sounds lifted above the low roar of the crowd and heads began to turn in their direction. Grant ducked his head, started to sip his drink, but decided it couldn't numb the ache inside him. Scowling, he shoved it away.

After a moment, Griffin sobered, gave his brother a silent toast and said, "So what are you going to do about it?"

"About what?"

"Annie."

"Nothing. Annie's gone. She left. There's nothing to do."

Griffin clapped him on the back. "You have a lot to learn, big brother, about women."

"Maybe." Maybe not. Maybe he didn't want to learn anything about women...about Annie. He knew enough already.

"Where'd she go?" Griffin asked.

"Home to Texas."

"And you're going to let her go?" Griffin shook his

head. "And you thought I was dumb to run out on her."

"She loved you last week," he said. "Who's to say she won't love somebody else next week?"

"Ah, she never really loved me," Griffin confessed.

"She gave a good show of it," Grant said, remembering that first kiss she'd given him when she'd thought he was Griffin.

"She loved the idea of me. She loved that I could get her out of Lockett." He cupped his hands around his glass. "But from the way she was eyeing you...well, she never looked at me that way. And for Annie, when she loves, she loves forever."

"How do you know?"

"Because I know Annie, just like you do." He smiled at Grant's appalled look. "No, not that way. We never...we were never intimate. She wanted to wait until our honeymoon. You know me though—I would have jumped in the sack on our first date. But Annie, well, she's a romantic."

She was. And he'd handled everything wrong.

Griffin clapped Grant on the back. "She's all yours, big brother. Now, how are you going to get her back?"

"I don't think she'd have me."

For the first time in his life, Grant was beginning to understand his little brother, understand why he became engaged then ran away on his frozen feet, understand his doubts. But Grant didn't just have doubts. He had fears. Giant fears. But not of Annie.

His fears had nothing to do with her—not anymore. His fear had everything to do with his upbringing, with the fading of love, with the fear that love wasn't enough.

"Why don't you give her a chance before you condemn her and yourself?"

"I don't want marriage," Grant said. "What else do I have to offer?"

"Well, you could start with your heart," Griffin said. "And marriage isn't so bad."

"Oh, yeah!" Grant gave a sputtering laugh. "Then how come you keep running from matrimony?"

"After I walked out on Annie, I had a lot of time to think. Marriage to her wouldn't be like our folks' marriage. Their love was conditional. If Dad bought Mom the right house, the right car, the right jewelry, then she was happy. If Mom fixed dinner on time, kept us kids in line, cleaned the house, then he was okay. That's a lot of ifs and a lot of doubt, and not enough love.

"But you and I know, Annie isn't that way. Love to her is forever."

"Or until the next groom walks in the door." The second the words escaped his mouth, Grant knew they were about his fears, not about Annie.

He had never imagined that his brother could be so intelligent, so introspective. But this time Griffin was right. When he thought of Annie, let his heart guide him, he knew she would love him unconditionally. It was when he let his fears and doubts creep into the picture that everything blurred and grayed.

Tossing a peanut at his brother, Grant declared, "I'm going after her."

Griffin nodded with a smile and reached into his jacket pocket. "Here. You'll need this then." He handed Grant a slip of paper.

"What is it?"

"My ticket to Dallas. Just make a connecting flight to Amarillo from there or drive the rest of the way on your own."

"Thanks, Griffin. I owe you."

They shook hands. It was the first time Grant could remember feeling a real connection with his brother.

"Nah," Griffin said. "Let's call it even."

IT TOOK five days and several phone calls before Grant made it to Annie's aunt Maudie's house. He stood in her parlor room pacing the carpeted floor, weaving between ornate antique furniture that made the small, overcrowded room even tinier. "What finally convinced you to let me come?"

Aunt Maudie placed a tray of finger sandwiches on the dining-room table. "Well, sugar, I must say you were persistent. That went in your favor. But, frankly, it had nothing to do with you. Annie convinced me."

"Annie? How?"

"I'm worried about her. Her appetite or her lack of appetite. I've never in my life seen her pass up fries from the D-Q or my cheese grits. Nope, I knew then she was smitten. The real thing this time."

"What time did you say she was going to be here?"

"After the guests arrive," Aunt Maudie said, giving the bench that sat in front of the bay window one last brush with the feather duster. "Don't you worry. She won't miss her party."

"What party? Is it her birthday?" He realized then he didn't even know when that was. But he'd find out, and he'd never forget. He knew what made her tick and that was what counted. And he knew he loved her.

"It's her going-away party."

"But she just got back."

"Long enough to pack her things and put the house on the market."

"Where's she going?" he asked, hoping Aunt Maudie wouldn't say Dallas or some other place.

"New York. She got a job there. Didn't she tell you?"

"Yeah." Relief spread through him. "Maybe I should have gone to her house."

Aunt Maudie shook her head. "No sirree. This will be better. It'll show those ol' biddies that Annie has found the right man for her."

"I don't care about any of her friends and neighbors and what they think." He'd heard enough at the airport before he'd taken Annie to New York with him. Grant tapped his pocket to make sure the wedding ring he'd bought for her was still safe.

"You will once you hear all they've been saying. A bunch of old crows. Nothin' better to do than caw about other folks' troubles."

"Why'd Annie tell them our marriage didn't work out?" Grant asked. "Why didn't she just continue with the charade until she'd left town for good?"

"Annie's that way. She's too honest. Besides, I don't think their yapping has been as hard on her as losing you."

Guilt arced through Grant. But her words also gave him hope that he wasn't too late. "You mean that?"

"Yes. I've never seen her so lackluster. And, believe

me, I've seen her grieve over her parents and stupid fiancés. Like I said, nothing has ever curbed her appetite. You know that's serious."

Damn. He didn't want her to suffer, but she'd refused all his phone calls. He'd considered driving straight here once he'd landed in Dallas Saturday night, but instead he'd decided to buy her a real ring, a ring that would show her how much he loved her. It would show everybody that she belonged to him. He'd picked the ring up on Tuesday and driven straight to Aunt Maudie's. Hell, if he was going to propose, he was going to do it right. And that meant getting permission from the most important person in Annie's life.

"Aunt Maudie," he said, feeling a sudden constriction in his throat, "I have to ask you something."

She looked up from placing pink napkins on the dining table beside the china plates. "Yes?"

He cleared his throat. "Uh, seeing that Annie's parents are deceased... And I know this doesn't really have to be done, but I'd feel a whole lot better following protocol..."

She walked over to him and laid a gentle hand on his arm. "Get to the point, Grant. I've got company coming any minute."

"Yes, ma'am. Well, I'd like to ask you, knowing that you're the most important person in Annie's life, for her hand in marriage."

Tears sprang to the older woman's eyes and she sniffed. "You're the first one who's ever done that." She wiped her tears with her apron. "None of her other fiancés bothered to ask formally. And that's probably why they found it so easy to break their promise. Don't you think?"

"I don't know. Aunt Maudie, ma'am, will you...give me your niece's hand in matrimony?"

"Oh, pish-posh! Of course I will!" She hugged him close and clapped him on the back.

Relief surged inside him. One down. One to go.

"But I have to tell you honestly, I don't know what she'll say to your proposal. Annie's been hurt and, well, I don't offer any guarantees with my blessing."

# 15

"HERE THEY COME!" Aunt Maudie announced, peeking out her sheer curtains. She shooed Grant toward the kitchen. "Now you stay put till Annie gets here."

"Why? You think she'd make a run for it?"

Aunt Maudie laughed. "She makes a good bride on the run."

"I don't want one on the run, I want one that'll stay put."

She patted Grant's back. "I hope she will. I surely hope she will."

A stream of women began arriving, parading through Aunt Maudie's house as if it was Easter. They held the china cups and doilied plates, their pinkies stuck straight out as they nipped at the finger sandwiches and sipped the orange tea without messing up their lipstick. Old women in flouncing dresses and younger women in more contemporary styles chattered like a flock of geese. Their laughter was polite and never too loud, the secretive comments whispered so as not to carry too far. But Grant overheard much as he peered around the swinging door from the kitchen.

A woman with a sagging neck and an ugly flowered hat shook her head, making the loose skin around her jowls waggle. "I'll never understand it. Why would she want to go to New York City? Her dear parents must be turning over in their graves."

"Oh, I think it'll suit her fine," said a younger woman who chewed with her mouth full. She swallowed then crammed another finger sandwich between her bright red lips. "Aren't they all a little nutty up there?"

The older woman set her cup on her plate. "You're probably thinking of those California fruitcakes."

"Oh, sure. But Yankees aren't much better."

"You're probably right."

"Annie never did fit in here. She's just too...too..." She waited as Aunt Maudie filled her cup with more tea and moved to the other end of the crushed-velvet sofa before finishing.

*Too spunky,* Grant thought. *Definitely too sexy for this crowd. Too smart to stay where she's not appreciated.*

"...different," the woman finally finished.

Grant rolled his eyes. This crowd was definitely unimaginative. But they were right. Annie didn't belong here.

"Probably why she couldn't ever keep a man," a blond woman said, leaning forward and tossing in her two worthless cents.

The women nodded in agreement.

Grant seethed. There was nothing wrong with Annie—except that she wasn't married to him. Yet.

ANNIE SAT on a chair, plastered on a tight smile and snuck a glance at her watch. She would endure this for Aunt Maudie's sake, for her mother's memory. And then she'd skip out of town and head to the airport where she'd begin her new life in New York City.

But the glamour and adventure no longer appealed to her. Neither did staying here. Fact was, nothing simmered with promise since Grant had broken her heart.

"Annie, you poor thing, you have had such sorry luck in love." Mrs. Sarks, the reverend's wife, patted Annie's knee. "Why, the last thing your mother said to me was that she hoped you would find some wonderful young man to love you as much as your father loved her."

Her heart pinched with the knowledge that she'd found the man, but he didn't love her the way she loved him. Maybe she should forget returning to New York, forget her new job and consider a convent.

"You better hurry then, Annie," Reverend Sarks's daughter-in-law, Melanie, said, "if you want him to be young."

Titters ruffled around the room. Annie felt stiff, her smile wooden. She wondered if she could catch an earlier flight.

"At least this last time she got her handsome fiancé to show up at the wedding and marry her."

"That's one thing we can all say is that Annie Baxter sure knows how to pick handsome men!"

"Land sakes, yes!"

"So what happened to this last one, Annie? How come your marriage didn't work out?" Mary Norton asked.

"Certainly didn't give it much time, did she?" someone whispered.

Annie had strategically told her next-door neighbor, who worked at the post office, the news that her marriage had failed after only one week. That way she wouldn't have to repeat it five thousand more times. She'd told only Aunt Maudie the truth.

Her aunt had held her as she'd cried out her frustrations, her sorrow, her pain. She'd listened as Annie had railed against Grant one minute and spoke of his many virtues and assets the next. But at night, she'd been left alone with her memories, her thoughts, her dreams. And they all revolved around Grant.

Her loneliness throbbed inside her. She dug a fingernail into her palm to distract herself and refocused on the neighbors who had gathered to say goodbye. Maybe she shouldn't have come back. Maybe she should have bought new furniture and clothes and asked Aunt Maudie to dispose of the rest.

But she'd needed to come back—to tell Aunt Maudie the truth and to say goodbye. She'd also wanted to pack up her mother's yellow daisy dishes and her father's well-loved books and take them with her. Those couldn't be replaced.

And neither could Grant.

"So, what was it?" someone else prompted. "Did he get bored during your honeymoon?"

"Where'd you go for your honeymoon anyway?" someone else asked.

Faces blurred, voices sounded as if they were underwater under the weight of tears that pressed against the backs of her eyes. She felt her heart collapsing with grief. Even the promise of a new life, a new home and lots of adventure couldn't pull her out of this dark depression. Only Grant could. But he didn't want her. After all, if he did, wouldn't he have followed her by now?

She looked around her aunt's home, the pastel silks and velvets, the dark, gleaming woods, the delicate china. Her aunt had made this her home with her knickknacks and beloved pieces of furniture, her own personal history. But Annie didn't have a home...or a future.

The house where she'd lived since she was born was packed and a For Sale sign was staked in the yard. The two-story didn't house the memories of her parents; her heart did. Lockett held nothing for her anymore. These neighbors weren't her friends; they simply liked to gossip about her exploits. Her new home would be in New York, but the apartment she'd secured late last week wouldn't be home, either. Because home was where the heart was. And her heart was definitely with Grant.

For so long she'd believed the grass was always greener in a different relationship...a new town... somewhere else. But it wasn't. Having to face her family and friends about her "failed marriage" had not been as difficult as facing her lonely bed each night.

"So, Annie," her high-school rival, Trisha Waters, said with a gloating expression, "couldn't you keep your man satisfied?"

A gasp ripped through the room.

Annie squared her shoulders, ready to tell the woman exactly what she'd done to please Grant. She knew it would blister a few ears around the room, but at least she'd wouldn't be forgotten quickly in Lockett.

"I wouldn't say that." A deep male voice startled the ladies, who all turned.

Stunned, Annie looked toward the door leading to the kitchen. Her breath snagged on the broken pieces of her heart. *Grant.*

"We had a fabulous honeymoon, didn't we, Annie?"

She nodded, unable to form a word or phrase in her head.

He walked toward her slowly and the waves of pink and lavender dresses parted. He wore faded jeans and a pale yellow button-down shirt, the sleeves rolled up midway to his elbows. His hair looked disheveled. He gave her a warm, disarming smile, and she felt whatever was left of her heart melt. She wanted to throw herself into his arms but she was unable to move, unable to accept that this wasn't some dream she'd conjured up out of desperation.

Then he knelt in front of her. He took her hand between his and his warmth flowed into her, made her realize this was real. He was real. *He was here!*

But what did it mean?

"What are you doing here?" she asked, her voice hoarse with emotion.

"I came to get you."

"But—"

"First, I came to apologize. I was wrong. I should have told you up front what you were getting into. I should have warned you about Susan."

Something inside Annie tightened, twisted, contracted.

"She is my difficult client. Difficult because we used to date."

"Grant, I don't want to know anything. I don't want to hear this."

"I do," somebody to her left whispered.

"I was worried," Grant said, "that she'd go with another investment banker if she learned of my feelings for you. It was wrong of me. And in the long run, whatever money I'll make with her account amounts to nothing if I don't have you."

His words punctured her anger. But she couldn't give in to the desire to fall into his arms. It wouldn't work. They were too different. She couldn't be all that he needed...or wanted.

"Can you forgive me?" he asked.

"Were you ashamed of me?" she asked, her voice pale.

"Hell, no. I was more ashamed that I'd dated her."

She looked down at their two hands joined. Their fingers laced through each other and she felt a fluttering deep inside her.

"Can you forgive me?" he asked, his voice dipping lower.

She looked up, saw the shimmer of tears at the corners of his eyes.

"I didn't mean to hurt you."

"I know." She cupped his hands with both of hers. "Yes, I forgive you."

"Good. Because I really want our marriage to work."

What was he saying? Was this just a continuation of their charade? Or had his apology been real? It had seemed genuine, but now confusion brought a surge of doubts. "Grant—"

"I'd marry you all over again, Annie. Would you marry me?"

"Grant—"

"Hell, I'd propose all over again, too."

Stunned, she watched as he pulled a jeweler's box out of his pocket, lifted the lid and showed her a sparkling marquis surrounded by two bands of diamonds. An *ahh* traveled around the room.

Annie's chest ached. "Why are you doing this?"

"Because I love you." His solemn gaze met hers. "I love you, Annie Baxter, and I can't live without you."

"No." She stood and moved away from him. She stepped around the ladies gathered there, crushing a few toes in her rush to get away from him. "I'm sorry, Grant. This isn't going to work."

In her peripheral vision, she saw heads shake and heard shocked gasps. She didn't care what they thought. This was her decision, her life!

"Annie—" Grant moved toward her.

"I said no and I meant it."

Aunt Maudie put her arm around Annie, supporting her decision. "Maybe this wasn't a good idea. Maybe you should go, Grant."

His gaze never left Annie. "Tell me why first."

"Why? Are you kidding? It can't work. It can't be right. It was too fast. I don't want to make any more mistakes. No, Grant. No. Now please go."

His eyes narrowed and his lips thinned. "Maybe it is right," he said in a low voice, making the women standing around the edges of the room lean forward to hear. But Annie heard each word clearly, distinctly. "Have you thought of that? Maybe it is right for all the right reasons this time."

"What do you mean?" someone else voiced the question Annie was too stubborn to ask herself.

"I mean that maybe part of you is as scared of marriage as I am...was."

"Why were you afraid?"

"I didn't exactly have good role models growing up. My folks always fought. Every week it seemed as if one or the other was threatening divorce." He shrugged, uncomfortable sharing the painful memories.

"That's horrible." Her eyes widened with empathy. "So hard on a child. It must have made your world very insecure."

"It's why I chose not to get married until now. And maybe fear is what made you choose fiancés who would walk out on you. Maybe deep down inside you knew it couldn't work with them."

"Grant, I don't want to be in love now. This is the wrong time. What if you decide to leave, too?"

"I'm not running." He stepped forward and pointed his finger at her chest. "You're the one that's running scared, Annie. And your fear is going to keep you from knowing how right it could have been if only you'd let us be together."

His face softened, and he touched her jaw, caressed her skin. Then he turned on his heel and strode out of Aunt Maudie's parlor, the roomful of pastel dresses parting like the Red Sea.

Annie felt her insides cave inward, collapse, as she

watched the man she loved walk out of her life. For good.

"Are you gonna just let that hunk of a man leave?"

"My, my, did you see that?"

"What must she be thinking?"

"See, I told you she's nuts!"

"You all hush now," Aunt Maudie scolded. "You just leave Annie alone. She's a full-grown woman capable of making her own decisions." In a softer tone, she asked, "You are sure about this, aren't you?"

No, she wasn't sure about anything.

Whispered words exploded around her in a cacophony of sound as the ladies jabbered back and forth about what had happened. Annie fingered her temple, pressed her fingertips into her skull. She needed to catch her breath. She had to think.

*My God! What did I do?*

Grant's parting words began to soak into the pieces of her heart and somehow mended it. Suddenly she realized the truth. The other men she was going to marry were a means of escape—to get out of Lockett, to find a new life. She had all that, all that and more. But she didn't have Grant. And she wanted him. She loved him.

She realized then that they had everything her other engagements had been missing—real, true storybook love. Blinking back her tears, she glanced out the bay window and saw Grant climbing into a blue pickup. She bolted for the door, threw it open and called, "Wait!"

He stopped and looked toward her.

"Grant!" She ran out onto the porch and stood on

the top step, hoping, praying he'd turn around and come back for her.

"Are you sure about this, Annie?" Aunt Maudie asked, coming out to join her.

"Yes, I am. I've never been so sure about anything in my life!"

"Well, then, darlin'—" Aunt Maudie kissed her cheek and hugged her close "—then I wish you every happiness. Now, go get your man!"

When Annie stepped away from her aunt, she stepped into Grant's arms. He held her for a long moment. He felt strong, solid, stable. She drew in the scent of him and looked up eager for his kiss.

But he had something else in mind. He knelt before her and took her hand in his. "This," he said, slipping the first band of diamonds on her finger, "is to represent the surprises and joy our first wedding brought to us." Then he slid the solitaire over her knuckle. "And this is for our engagement which will be very short."

Their eyes met, and she wondered just how quickly they would get married.

"And this—" he held up the second band of diamonds, "—is for our second wedding."

"Our second...?"

"If you'll have me, then I want to marry you this afternoon."

"This afternoon?" she echoed. Okay, their engagement would be even shorter than she'd imagined— roughly four hours.

He nodded. "There will be no delays, no cold feet, no backing out. This wedding will have to last us a lifetime."

Wrapping her arms around his neck, she said, "That's the best proposal I've ever received."

"And she should know," someone whispered, reminding Annie they weren't alone.

With a sunlit smile, she gave Grant a soul-searing kiss. At first, silence ricocheted along Aunt Maudie's porch, the ladies looking on with a reverence for romance. Then they began to shift uncomfortably as the kiss heated up. Annie vowed they'd never forget this kiss. Neither would she. And neither would Grant.

Then he whisked her up into his arms and carried her out to his rented pickup. The women fluttered after them, Aunt Maudie clicking pictures, the others eager to see all.

"I've got reservations," Grant said, "for us to fly to Vegas. Our wedding is scheduled for late this afternoon. I know it's not the most romantic place but—"

"It sounds heavenly, Grant," she sighed, hugging him tight.

"Why does she keep calling him Grant?" someone asked from Aunt Maudie's porch. "I thought his name was Griffin."

"Must be a nickname," someone else said. "Is she saying Grant or Granite?"

"Maybe he's hard as—"

"Ladies, please!" Aunt Maudie interrupted.

Grant and Annie shared a smile and another kiss as he settled her into the passenger seat. "Your wedding dress is in the back, along with my tux."

"Oh, Grant!"

"Believe me, darlin', we're going to do this right."

She scooted over to the middle so she'd be snug

against his side all the way to Amarillo...and for the rest of their lives.

As the truck started, Annie's aunt faced the women gawking on her front porch. "And for your information, his name's not Griffin. It's Grant Stevens. He's the groom's twin brother." She waved her handkerchief in farewell. "Now that ought to give this town something to talk about for years to come. Looks like my Annie has found the right man...and kept him!"

## HARLEQUIN® Temptation.

## Get ready to feel the

## with Temptation!

### Each and every month look for the hottest reads in the lineup!

**#829 *SEX APPEAL***
***Lori Foster*** (May)

**#835 *INSATIABLE***
***Julie Elizabeth Leto*** (June)

**#839 *SMOOTH MOVES***
***Carrie Alexander*** (July)

## *Feel the passion! Feel the excitement! Feel the*

**Fantasies Inc.**

*An exclusive agency that caters to
intimate whims, provocative requests
and decadent desires...*

*Four lush island resorts waiting to
transport guests into a private world of
sensual adventures, erotic pleasures
and seductive passions...*

*A miniseries that will leave readers
breathless and yearning for more...*

Don't miss:
#832 *SEDUCTIVE FANTASY* by Janelle Denison
*Available May 2001*

#836 *SECRET FANTASY* by Carly Phillips
*Available June 2001*

#840 *INTIMATE FANTASY* by Julie Kenner
*Available July 2001*

#844 *WILD FANTASY* by Janelle Denison
*Available August 2001*

# Do you have a secret fantasy?

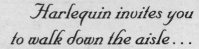

## Harlequin invites you to walk down the aisle...

To honor our year long celebration of weddings, we are offering an exciting opportunity for you to own the Harlequin Bride Doll. Handcrafted in fine bisque porcelain, the wedding doll is dressed for her wedding day in a cream satin gown accented by lace trim. She carries an exquisite traditional bridal bouquet and wears a cathedral-length dotted Swiss veil. Embroidered flowers cascade down her lace overskirt to the scalloped hemline; underneath all is a multi-layered crinoline.

Join us in our celebration of weddings by sending away for your own Harlequin Bride Doll. This doll regularly retails for $74.95 U.S./approx. $108.68 CDN. One doll per household. Requests must be received no later than December 31, 2001. Offer good while quantities of gifts last. Please allow 6-8 weeks for delivery. Offer good in the U.S. and Canada only. Become part of this exciting offer!

**Simply complete the order form and mail to:**
**"A Walk Down the Aisle"**

<u>IN U.S.A</u>
P.O. Box 9057
3010 Walden Ave.
Buffalo, NY 14269-9057

<u>IN CANADA</u>
P.O. Box 622
Fort Erie, Ontario
L2A 5X3

**Enclosed are eight (8) proofs of purchase found in the last pages of every specially marked Harlequin series book and $3.75 check or money order (for postage and handling). Please send my Harlequin Bride Doll to:**

_____
Name (PLEASE PRINT)

_____
Address                                    Apt. #

_____
City            State/Prov.         Zip/Postal Code

_____
Account # (if applicable)              **097 KIK DAEW**

HARLEQUIN®
*Makes any time special* ®

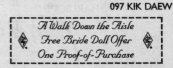

*A Walk Down the Aisle*
*Free Bride Doll Offer*
*One Proof-of-Purchase*

Visit us at www.eHarlequin.com                    PHWDAPOPR2

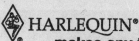

*Three sizzling love stories
by today's hottest writers
can be found in...*

# Midnight Fantasies....

*Feel the heat!*

*Available June 2001*

### MYSTERY LOVER—Vicki Lewis Thompson

When an unexpected storm hits, rancher Jonas Garfield
takes cover in a nearby cave...and finds himself seduced
senseless by an enigmatic temptress who refuses to tell him
her name. All he knows is that this sexy woman wants him.
And for Jonas, that's enough—for now....

### AFTER HOURS—Stephanie Bond

Michael Pierce has always considered costume shop
owner Rebecca Valentine no more than an associate—
until he drops by her shop one night and witnesses the
mousy wallflower's transformation into a seductive siren.
Suddenly he's desperate to know her much better.
But which woman is the real Rebecca?

### SHOW AND TELL—Kimberly Raye

A naughty lingerie party. A forbidden fantasy. When Texas
bad boy Dallas Jericho finds a slip of paper left over from
the party, he is surprised—and aroused—to discover that he
is good girl Laney Merriweather's wildest fantasy. So what
can he do but show the lady what she's been missing....

# INDULGE IN A QUIET MOMENT
# WITH HARLEQUIN

### Get a FREE
## *Quiet Moments*
## *Bath*
## *Spa*

### with just two proofs of purchase from
### any of our four special collector's editions in May.

---

**Harlequin® is sure to make your time special this Mother's Day
with four special collector's editions featuring a short story
*PLUS* a complete novel packaged together in one volume!**

Collection #1 Intrigue abounds in a collection featuring *New York Times*
bestselling author Barbara Delinsky and Kelsey Roberts.

Collection #2 Relationships? Weddings? Children? = *New York Times*
bestselling author Debbie Macomber and Tara Taylor Quinn
at their best!

Collection #3 Escape to the past with *New York Times* bestselling author
Heather Graham and Gayle Wilson.

Collection #4 Go West! With *New York Times* bestselling author
Joan Johnston and Vicki Lewis Thompson!

## *Plus Special Consumer Campaign!*

Each of these four collector's editions will feature a
"FREE QUIET MOMENTS BATH SPA" offer.
See inside book in May for details.

### Only from

**HARLEQUIN®**
*Makes any time special* ®

Don't miss out! Look for this exciting promotion on sale in May 2001,
at your favorite retail outlet.

Visit us at www.eHarlequin.com                    PHNCP01